HIGH-OCTANE
HEROES

HIGH-OCTANE HEROES

EROTIC ROMANCE FOR WOMEN

EDITED BY
DELILAH DEVLIN

FOREWORD BY
MAYA BANKS

CLEIS
PRESS

Published in the United States by Cleis Press, Inc., 2246 Sixth Street, Berkeley, California 94710.

Printed in the United States.
Cover design: Scott Idleman/Blink
Cover photograph: S. Shipman/Getty Images
Text design: Frank Wiedemann

First Edition.
10 9 8 7 6 5 4 3 2 1

Trade paper ISBN: 978-1-57344-969-4
E-book ISBN: 978-1-57344-981-6

Contents

FOREWORD

High-Octane Heroes. What does that say to you as a reader of romance? If you immediately get a smile and that warm, tingly, *sigh* feeling, then yeah, you're like me. You're happy. You know you're in for a treat.

What would romance be without the hot alpha male? Particularly the military man, the man in uniform. Along with that uniform, honor, loyalty and the undying willingness to protect, what would romance be without him? I don't know, and I don't particularly care to find out.

When asked to write a foreword for an anthology devoted to that kind of man, I knew that, yeah, I could do it, but how to put into words how I feel about that kind of hero? The kind of man I write for all of my books? A uniform is just that. Clothing. It's what is underneath that uniform that matters.

Whether the outer trappings are an actual uniform with a flag or a badge, or plain street clothes, or even a kilt or grungy, tight-fitting jeans, it's the man wearing them and the heart within him that is all-important to the reader.

We're romance readers. We want heart. We want heat. We want a guy who'll go to the wall every single time for his heroine and also the people important to him. Protect the innocent. Fight the good fight. Go to the wall. Every. Damn. Time.

If you like this kind of hero, if he hits every one of your reader buttons, then this is an anthology for you. A collection devoted solely to *that* kind of man. The super-alpha male, regardless of what—or any—uniform he wears. Ever hear the saying the clothes make the man? That's total crap. It's the heart that makes the man.

Maya Banks

INTRODUCTION

Without spelling out how long ago it actually was, I'll admit to an *early* fascination with manly men and their high-testosterone adventures. I loved cops, firemen, soldiers, knights in shining armor and spies. Remember "The Man from Uncle"? How about "The Saint"? Truth be told, I often imagined myself as a damsel in need of rescue, blonde hair flowing, hands tied and stretched above my head, my body at the mercy of a drooling fiend, and then the hero—once he'd dispatched the heinous villain. I'm sure you'll be relieved to know that although I always managed in those daydreams to somehow lose my clothes, I had only a very vague idea of what exactly the hero would do with me at that point. The rescue, the steamy glances and teasing caresses were enough to spur those young fantasies.

When I grew older and experienced some of those high-octane adventures for myself, I decided I didn't like imagining myself a victim, but instead standing toe to toe with that powerful male—until the moment he convinced me I'd really rather bend to his will...and wicked hands and mouth...

So when my editor asked me for ideas for another collection, I submitted my own personal fantasy, this idea of "high-octane" heroes, and although she took some convincing, my enthusiasm ultimately persuaded her that maybe there were other women out there who shared the same passion for those strong, studly men.

How lucky are we that so many writers knew exactly what I wanted? Maybe it was the description I gave when I announced my call for submissions...

What is it about heroes like Superman, Iron Man or Thor that revs our engines like no other? Is it the suit? The manly physique? Or is it the courage they display, wading in where others fear to go, to save the damsel, the city, the Earth?

Are there real-life heroes who inspire the same lustful fascination? Kick-ass iconic heroes who enter danger zones in the name of duty, honor, country—or maybe love—who conjure images of hard, chiseled bodies, deadly glares and camouflaged features?

I'll admit I got a little carried away there. Still, it worked.

I received stories of military men and everyday heroes within our own communities—policemen, personal trainers, firemen and even an EMT. While many of the stories feature women in need of rescue, many more show women ready to do the rescuing, to serve and defend their community, country and the world, while waging very sexy battles with those absurdly manly men.

Delilah Devlin

AS YOU WERE

Alice Janell

The rainfall of rocks and debris were the least of her problems. Someone shouted something, but the words were drowned in the sharp reports of weapons. Ears ringing from the spray of bullets not too far away, Laura kept focused on the injured solider in front of her. Heart pounding, she suppressed her fear and continued to work. A tourniquet had been tied off. If she could get him to the surgical unit quickly, maybe they could save his leg. If not...

Stay positive. It's just like training. Only he could die.

A rough hand jerked her away from her work.

"Stand down!" she barked, not even glancing at the soldier who distracted her momentarily.

"The med trucks are here. We have to go *now*. They've given the orders to pull out."

A quick glance at the uniform in front of her gave her a name: Stevens. Glancing up at the dirty face in front of her, she shook her head. "I'm not leaving him. Can you carry him?"

A quick nod from Stevens was all she needed. With her wounded soldier being carted toward the med trucks, she began to follow. An agonized groan caught her ear. How she heard it, she didn't know. The mixture of gunfire and shouts was deafening. She paused, looking. Stevens stopped.

"Go," she told him. "I'm right behind you."

Another quick survey of the area revealed nothing. Had she imagined it?

It happened in slow motion.

A bulldozer knocked her off her feet. *Something* hit the ground. Too close. Adrenaline coursed through her, and she tried to roll to the side, wanting to sprint toward the remaining trucks. But the bulldozer prevented her from doing anything. Rocks scattered around them, and she instinctively curled, ducking her head beneath her arms.

"I'm right here, Laura," a voice boomed in her ears. *Tony.*

She relaxed just a fraction as the sound of his voice washed over her. Before she could say anything to him, the sound of helicopters roared overhead. The cavalry had arrived. They needed to get out of the area. Fast.

Tony Valdez, the bulldozer of a soldier who'd tackled her to the ground, caught her gaze. His face was covered in dirt and grime, but that didn't matter. With his chiseled jaw and dark, penetrating gaze, Tony had her insides melting, even in the heat of battle. The look on his face, however, was all business. He motioned toward the remaining trucks. She nodded, knowing they were going to have to run at a dead sprint to catch them before they left.

A heartbeat passed. Then another.

Tony lifted his body off of hers, offered a hand to pull her up and began running. Laura followed suit, her hand still inside his. He was faster, able to take longer strides, but he stayed with

her. Soldiers in the trucks were waving, calling them to hurry.
Her adrenaline spiked, pumping her legs faster. A wisp of hair fell in her eyes, but she ignored it. Her muscles burned, but there wasn't time to think about that. She could rest later.

Tony jumped into the truck first, pulling her up after.

She started to thank him, but he shook his head.

"Later," he told her, taking a seat on the other side of the truck. He was panting, his face slick with sweat. He kept his gaze on her a moment longer and then closed his eyes.

As the truck sped away from the battle, she looked at the men and women around her. Each of them were haggard but all of them alive. She spared a brief thought for Stevens and her wounded soldier. She hoped they had made it to the med truck in time.

"Excuse me, ma'am?" Someone tapped her shoulder. "Are you a medic?"

She nodded. "Are you hurt?"

"No, ma'am —"

"Sergeant Hayes," she corrected.

"Sergeant Hayes," the boy repeated. He was a boy, too. He couldn't have been more than twenty with that baby face. "It's Tom—I mean, Corporal Briggs." He pointed to another young man sitting a few feet away, clutching his side and hissing through his teeth.

She nodded once and moved down toward Briggs. "Corporal, can you speak?"

"Yes." His voice was rough.

Laura could tell the effort hurt him. "Are you bleeding?"

"Nothing too serious. A few cuts. Hurts to breathe."

Placing her hand over his, she moved it and felt along his rib cage. When he cringed and shied from her touch she clucked her tongue. "Probably a bruised or fractured rib," she told him.

"There's not much I can do for you here, I'm afraid. Just keep as still as possible, taken even breaths. A doc can give you pain meds, but it should heal on its own in about six weeks."

Briggs nodded, relaxing a little. "Thanks, Sergeant."

After Briggs, Laura checked the other soldiers around her. None were seriously injured, thank goodness. Most had a few scrapes and cuts, and one had a gash on his forehead, but that was the extent of the injuries.

When she knelt in front of Tony, his eyes opened. There was a dark, predatory look in his eyes that sent shivers across her skin. She wished they were alone. She wanted to climb onto his lap, straddle his hips and feel his cock slide deep into her wet pussy. She licked her lips, her heart pounding in her chest. The corner of his mouth turned upward, a small smirk that told her he knew what she was thinking.

Tentatively, she placed a hand on his knee and hoped the others were either not paying attention or would assume she was merely checking him for injuries.

He brought his hand, calloused and rough, over hers. He held it there a moment too long, his deep brown eyes locked onto hers, before he moved her hand aside gently. "I'm fine, Sergeant." He used his gruff, professional soldier's voice, but his eyes sparkled, a secret look meant only for her. The heat she felt had nothing to do with the desert sun or the bodies packed into the back of the rattling truck.

His balls tightened.

Glancing down at her hand on his knee, fingers splayed across his thigh, Tony gritted his teeth when she began prodding softly against his muscle, presumably looking for injuries. He tensed and caught her hand in his before her touch could wander farther.

"I'm fine, Sergeant." His voice was low and demanding. If she continued to touch him, even in a clinical, nonsexual way, he didn't think he could refrain from touching her back. Holding her gaze, he imagined her leaning forward, those pouty pink lips parting, her tongue darting toward the head of his cock. His dick stirred.

She held his gaze for a moment, and Tony wondered if she saw the desire in his eyes. She arched a slender blonde eyebrow, blue eyes searching his. He kept his gaze on her as she nodded once and moved to her own seat. Watching Laura, he thought of things he wanted to do to her, the ways he wanted to take her. He closed his eyes, letting his mind wander to sinful fantasies. His cock hardened; his balls grew painfully tight. Gritting his teeth, he looked out the back of the truck, watching the desert stretch endlessly into the distance. So long as he didn't meet her eyes, then maybe his case of blue balls would go away.

He doubted it.

The ride back to camp was blessedly uneventful, only the sound of the soldiers' gear jostling and Briggs's occasional groans of pain breaking the silence. It was good to be in civilization. Or as close to civilization as base got, anyway.

Laura spared him a quick glance as she was rushed toward the hospital unit. Of course she'd want to check on the soldier she'd been treating.

Damn it.

He'd meant to pull her aside and ask her when she'd have a spare moment for a quick fuck.

Tony didn't mind rubbing one off, but the thought of thrusting his cock into her wet pussy was a hundred times more enticing than a bottle of lotion and his right hand.

Someone ahead of him barked orders. Thoughts of Laura pushed aside, he stood at attention with the rest of the men from the truck. He knew the routine. They would be sent to the hospital unit to be checked for injuries. The thought brought a smile to his lips. Maybe he could find Laura and ask her about a rendezvous after all.

At the hospital, Tony was ushered into a room. After a long wait a medic came in, checked him for injuries and left. He sighed and sank down on the bed. He wondered how long it would take for the doc to come back and clear him to leave. He wanted to find Laura.

She found him first.

"How are you feeling?" she asked, entering his room.

"Tired, but I'll live. A few cuts and a couple of bruises." He estimated that it had been almost five hours since he had pulled Laura out of that nightmare. Since the grenade had been thrown. It was a miracle they'd escaped with only minor injuries. "You?"

She smiled, her blue eyes softening. Her hand was cool and smooth as she placed it over his. "I'm fine. A little sore but nothing a little R&R can't cure." Laura cleared her throat, her hand withdrawing.

Tony watched as her features changed. The small, secretive smile becoming a thin, tight line. He recognized the change. She wasn't Laura, the woman he was sleeping with. She was Sergeant Hayes, the combat medic checking in on the soldiers she'd treated in the field. Though she hadn't treated him, he was glad to see her. She'd showered, and he was envious. Her face was fresh and clean, her blonde hair pulled back into a tight bun at the nape of her neck. She'd changed out of her ACUs and into a pair of green scrubs. The thin cotton material hinted at her feminine curves. He knew she was tanned and toned with a neatly trimmed nest of dark gold curls at the apex of her thighs.

He watched as she flipped through his chart—everyone

in the truck had been admitted to the hospital to ensure no serious, hidden physical damage had been done. He thought it was stupid, but even he couldn't go against a doctor's orders.

"Doc says you're free to go," she said, setting the clipboard down at the foot of the bed.

He stood, gaze darting toward the door of his room. She had closed it. Good. Clever girl. His earlier fantasies clouded his mind. He had to have her.

He looked back to Laura. "Sergeant Hayes."

"Yes, Staff Sergeant?" she asked, pressing her lips together. Was she hiding a smile?

"When can I see you?" Straight and to the point. No bullshitting with Laura. She didn't like small talk any more than he did. He liked that about her.

"You're seeing me right now, Staff Sergeant."

She was teasing him.

He took two steps, crossing the short distance between them. The faint scent of Ivory soap and shampoo taunted him. Tantalized him with fantasies of tasting her clean skin. Her gaze lifted, looking up at him from beneath dark lashes.

With one hand, he cupped the nape of her neck, wishing her hair was loose and he could tangle his fingers in the silky tresses. His lips descended on hers, the kiss rough and ravenous.

She backed into the wall with a gasp, her tongue probing his.

His cock was rock hard in seconds. With his free hand, he grasped her breast, massaging it with his fingers.

"Tony," she whispered between kisses. "Not here, Tony."

With a growl and a string of muttered curses, he pulled his mouth away from hers and stepped back. She was right. He was a higher rank, and their relationship could be seen as fraternization. Neither he nor Laura wanted to deal with the paperwork that came with wanting to reveal their relationship. They'd agreed to keep their meetings secret. Fucking on a hospital bed was out of the question.

He was insatiable. She loved that about him.

Her lips tingled, remembering the feel of his mouth on hers, hot and hungry.

If the door had a lock she might have let him take her right then and there. But the hospital was too risky. Although they were technically within their rights to pursue a relationship, the military was funny about such things. Sexual relationships on deployments were frowned upon. To avoid the headache, she and Tony shared many stolen kisses and quickies in closets.

However, the aching need building between her legs told Laura that a quickie wasn't going to cut it. Not this time.

"Are they really making you work so soon after?" he asked in that gruff masculine voice of his.

She shook her head. "No, of course not. I was debriefed and given a ninety-six. I really wanted a shower and the hospital is closer than my barracks. Plus," she added, her gaze falling to his lips briefly, "I wanted to see you."

A half-truth. She'd wanted to check on her wounded soldier, first. The doctors had saved his leg and the soldier had thanked her. It was only after checking on him that she thought to find Tony.

"Laura," Tony groaned, his voice ragged.

"I know," she said quietly. The ache was a dull throb, still demanding the feel of his hard shaft and the sweet relief of an orgasm.

"Meet me at my barracks in two hours."

She blinked. Their base had more amenities than most, and Tony shared his room with one other soldier. Even if he could manage time in his room alone, there was no *good* reason for a female to be wandering around an all-male barracks. The harassment and mortification of other men whistling and catcalling wouldn't bother her, but if anyone recognized her or saw her slip into Tony's room alone...

Getting caught could put both their careers in jeopardy.

"Find an excuse," he told her before she could protest. "Lab results. X-rays. Anything."

"But Tony, if we're caught..."

He closed the gap between them in a long stride. His lips fell on hers, rough and insistent, stealing her breath. His body was hard and all muscle, and the feel of him against her, coupled with his kiss, only fanned the fire between her legs. When he pulled away, she panted for breath.

"Two hours," he repeated as he walked away from her to exit the hospital room. "Find an excuse."

His eyes glittered darkly and for a moment, Laura wondered what would happen if she didn't show up.

"And if I can't?" she asked, her voice a breathy whisper.

He smirked. "Then I'll come to your room and fuck your brains out."

He left then, closing the door with a soft click behind him. He wouldn't come to her room, not really, she thought. Not when she shared a room with five other women. But then again, she'd never seen Tony quite so aroused. Yet, it was a scintillating thought, and the risk of going to his barracks only heightened her own arousal.

She took a few moments to compose herself before leaving the room. She had two hours to come up with an excuse to be at his barracks. It took an hour before she came up with something. She couldn't take real lab results or X-rays, but she could make copies of the ones used for training purposes.

Fifteen minutes before her two hours were up, she strode

into the all-male barracks in green scrubs and a white lab coat she'd commandeered. A brown folder was tucked under her arm stuffed with fake medical reports. Tony was sitting at the duty desk, freshly showered and clean shaven.

"Where —" she began, wanting to ask where the actual duty officer was.

"Taking a piss," he said, slipping a small gold key into her hand. "Down the hall, second door on the right. Quick."

She darted down the hall and entered his room. This room, like all the others, she suspected, was simple: a toilet and sink, two closets, two desks and two neatly made beds.

She jumped as the door opened a few minutes later.

"Just me," Tony teased.

She sighed. "You scared the shit out of me."

"Sounds like you need to relax," he commented, wrapping an arm around her waist and pulling her against him. The fake file fell from her arm, pages scattering at their feet.

"Your roommate?"

"Gone for the next few hours. Grabbing chow, calling his family."

He kissed her. Unlike before, this kiss was soft and sensual.

Her shoulders fell, her body relaxing in his arms. Wrapping her arms around his neck, she parted her lips, her tongue dancing against his as the kiss deepened. Slowly, he led her toward his bed, his lips moving from her lips to her jaw and to the sweet spot just below her ear.

Pulling away from him, she watched as he began undoing the buttons of his ACUs, the camouflaged jacket sliding off his body and onto the floor. He sat on his roommate's bed, eyes watching her as she, too, began to strip off her clothing. He undid the laces of his boots, kicked them off and began loosening the belt at his waist.

Her heart raced as he lifted his green T-shirt over his head, her eyes following the lines and contours of his muscular torso. Pulling her hair free from its bun, she lifted her own shirt and began slipping her arms through the straps of her functional white bra.

"Fuck you have gorgeous tits," he said, eyes on her breasts as he took a step toward her, cupping a breast in one hand. A calloused thumb grated gently across her nipple, the sensation causing her to gasp.

Slowly, she slid her hands up his thick biceps, tilted her head and offered her neck to his lips.

With his roommate gone for the next three hours, he took his time, savoring the taste of Laura's clean skin, the soft sweet scent of her soap and feminine musk. Taking his hand from her breast, he trailed his kisses across her collarbone and down her breast until he could rake his teeth across her nipple. His hands slid down her flat stomach, fingers dipping beneath the hem of her pants.

Scrubs were easily pulled away, the elastic stretching as he began removing her pants. Her hips undulated, assisting him, and Tony couldn't help but slide his palm across her tight ass, the white cotton panties she wore a thin barrier that taunted him.

Still lavishing her nipple with attention from his mouth and tongue, he bit down delicately on the hard nub. When she moaned, his cock twitched.

It had been too long since he'd had her beneath him, eager, willing and waiting for him. He pressed her back, until she sat and slid her legs onto his narrow bed. He straightened, smirking when she whimpered in disappointment. Pulling his pants down, he kept his eyes locked on hers.

.

Beneath his boxer-briefs his dick was hard, waiting to spring free. Blue eyes dark and dreamy, Laura tucked her thumbs into the elastic of her panties, wriggling on the mattress as the white fabric slid down her thighs. With a seductive smile, she pinched a nipple between her thumb and forefinger before sliding her hand down her body toward the neatly trimmed tangle of golden curls. His gaze darted to her face for a moment. As she watched him, she slid two fingers into her pussy.

The erotic sight of Laura touching herself on his bed had his heart beating hard in his chest. Her fingers pumped in and out of her wet channel, and she exhaled a soft groan.

"Tony," she whispered, her eyes still fixated on him. "Fuck me."

He didn't need a second invitation.

As he removed his boxer-briefs, his cock stood at attention, and Laura smiled when she saw it. "Come here, soldier," she said with a sexy curl of her finger.

"Are you giving an order to a superior?" he asked, reaching into his bedside table for a condom.

"You're damn right I am." She smiled, her hand grasping his cock in a firm grip. Her fingers were slick from her pussy, and the feel of her wetness on his dick doubled his desire for her. Her hand pumped his dick a couple of times, her fingertips brushing against his balls.

Tearing the foil packet open with his teeth, Tony rolled the condom onto his dick and climbed onto the bed, his body looming over hers. Weaving his hands through her silky blonde hair, he tugged just hard enough to tilt back her neck. He kissed the sensitive flesh, once again trailing his kisses down to her breasts. Grasping his hard shaft in his other hand, he nudged her slick folds, parting them enough to tease her.

"Oh!" she gasped, her back arching.

"Not yet, darling," he said, chuckling.

She murmured a protest, but brought her hips back down. Sliding his cock across her pussy was just as much torture for him as it was for her, but he loved to make her beg. He rubbed the head of his cock against her clit, then her wet opening. He pushed in just a fraction of an inch.

"God, Tony," she pleaded. "Do it."

"Say it." He pulled away.

"Oh god, just do it."

He pushed against her slick folds again. "Say it."

"Please..." Her hips rolled, attempting to capture his dick.

"You can do better than that," he said, his voice deepening in pleasure.

"Fuck me, baby. Please."

Laura cried out when his cock plunged into her forcefully. He let out a low groan as the walls of her pussy adjusted to accommodate his thick girth as he began thrusting in a steady rhythm. He took her mouth; his hands eagerly explored her body. The rough feel of his fingertips sliding across her skin sent shivers down her spine.

Flesh against flesh, the heat between them produced a light sheen of sweat on their bodies. Laura dug her nails into his back, raking them down his spine, marking him with scratches. His cock drove deeper into her, and she rolled her hips against him, expressing her growing need. She tugged at his lower lip with her teeth, and the snarl he emitted from his throat was deep and dangerous.

Tension began to build, ready to spill over the edge and into oblivion, but before bliss could be achieved, Tony pulled out his cock, leaving her pussy pulsing with the need to climax.

"Turn over," he ordered, his voice harsh and ragged.

Obliging, she turned, her hair falling like a curtain over her face.

His hands gripped her ass; fingers splayed across the smooth skin. She felt his cock poised at her entrance. Then he pushed into her pussy from behind.

Laura gripped plain white sheets as he began pounding into her hard. She bit her lip to keep from crying out, the feel of his rough thrusting driving her closer and closer to the edge. His hands were on her hips, guiding her back and forth as he pumped furiously. Her nerves grew taut, like a rubber band stretched too tightly.

She snapped.

Her orgasm was explosive, coursing through her body like the aftershock of an earthquake. She cried out his name, riding wave after wave of pleasure as it rippled through her.

Reaching a hand around her hip, Tony played with her clit as he continued to thrust.

Too sensitive, she bucked against him until his deep breathing turned into short grunts. He stilled behind her, the two of them panting and reveling in the aftermath of their orgasms.

He drew away and she rolled onto her back, willing her heart to slow its furious beating. Once she'd caught her breath, she sat up.

"So," she said with a smile as she reached for her panties and scrubs. "Any ideas on how you're going to smuggle me out of here?"

A hand reached for her wrist and tightened like a manacle around it. "Honey, I'm alone for a couple more hours yet," he said, his voice a husky drawl. "You think I'm letting you leave right now?"

She glanced sideways, biting her bottom lip. "I do need a way out of here, you know. Whether it's now or in two hours."

"You leave that to me. In the meantime…"

She arched a slender eyebrow as his voice trailed off, desire glittering in his wicked, dark eyes. A quick glance at his hardening cock, and she could see he was nearly ready to go again.

"Yes, Staff Sergeant?" Her voice was sweet with mock innocence.

He grinned, teeth flashing white against his tanned skin as he nodded for her to lie back on his bed. "As you were, soldier."

FIVE-ALARM
FIRE

Sabrina York

The call came in just as Luke Patterson and his partner Izzy were sitting down to a big bowl of Five-Alarm Chili. Mrs. Lipniki was having another heart attack.

"Whaddya think, Luke?" Izzy quipped, as he leapt into the passenger side of the paramedic unit. "Is it the real deal this time or just another false alarm?"

Luke responded with a one-shouldered shrug. They both knew it was a rhetorical question. Mrs. Lipniki was, after all, a regular. They suspected she called as often as she did because she was lonely, but lately things had changed. Lately, she'd been calling in emergencies to try and set them up with her granddaughters.

And her nieces.

And her cousin's uncle's nephew's sister.

As they roared down the main street of town, heading for the little duplex they knew so well, Luke swallowed his cynicism. One of these days Mrs. Lipniki might really have a heart attack; it was his job to make sure she got the best possible care, no matter what.

"Hokay," Izzy muttered as they pulled into the driveway. "Lock and load."

They jetted from the truck, grabbed the portable defibrillator and their EMT bag, and double-timed it to the door. It stood open. Without preamble, they moved into place.

While Izzy unpacked the defibrillator, Luke knelt beside Mrs. Lipniki and started taking her vitals. As he placed the cold cup of his stethoscope against her chest, she flinched and bit back a tiny smile.

Luke and Izzy exchanged a look. *False alarm.* Again.

Still and all, they always followed protocol. Always.

Luke turned to the young woman kneeling quietly beside his patient. And almost swallowed his tongue. Holy shit, she was gorgeous. Her face had classic lines, an adorable snub nose, and a cleft chin—the kind that drove him crazy.

And her body? Curves that fucking didn't quit. A far cry from last week's emaciated offering. Hunger snarled through him. He fixed his features into a dispassionate expression. "Can you tell us what happened?"

She glanced up and, through the shadows, their gazes met. Luke blinked, a little stunned. She had the most beautiful eyes he'd ever seen. A deep-violet sea fringed in thick black lashes. He could drown in that ocean.

"She just grabbed her chest and fell to the floor."

Luke barely registered the words. Her musical voice sent shards of lust dancing along his nerve endings—all the way to his cock.

He forced himself to focus. "D-did she hit her head when she fell?"

"No."

Luke had to look away; she was far too distracting. He wasn't here to meet chicks—not even magnificent, violet-eyed vixens. Regardless of Mrs. Lipniki's evil plans.

He nodded, businesslike, and strapped the blood pressure cuff to his patient's limp arm. As he began to pump air into the cuff, Mrs. Lipniki moaned. She usually regained consciousness about then because she hated having her blood pressure taken.

"Oh!" she warbled in an operatic tenor. "Luke, is that you?" Since she was a little hard of hearing, she had a tendency to yell—even when she warbled.

"Yes, Mrs. Lipniki," he said wryly. "I'm right here. How are you feeling?"

"I feel faint." She affected the classic "tragedy pose" with the backs of her fingers to her brow.

"Oh dear," the sweet female to Luke's side murmured. Low and resonant, her words had an uncomfortable effect in his trousers. "Will she be all right?"

"Trish?" The old lady thrashed her hand about madly, eyes still screwed shut. "Is that you?"

Wisely, Trish captured that flailing appendage and held it close. "I'm right here, sweetie."

"Oh Trish...Trish." Mrs. Lipniki rolled toward Luke, cracked open one eye and bellowed in a conspiratorial tone, "Trish is my neighbor." And then, just below a dull roar, "She's *single*. A *good* girl."

The good girl's mouth fell open. A delicate blush lit her cheeks. She looked mortified.

Relentless, Mrs. Lipniki turned her gimlet gaze on poor Trish. "Luke is a *fireman*. He's a very nice *boy*. His hands are very *large*." She lifted one up, just to show poor Trish, waggling it around like a flopping trout.

Luke could hear Izzy snickering behind him, but he didn't care.

Because Trish was smiling.

It was a small smile, kind of shy, but she was luminous. Dimples exploded in her cheeks.

"Oh, you two would be perfect together." Mrs. Lipniki wheezed, as though on her last breath. She clutched at her chest. "You should go on a *date*."

Trish gasped. "Mrs. Lipniki! That's…" Her gaze met Luke's. "Silly."

"Is it?" he asked in an undertone, slowly winding his stethoscope and tucking it into his bag.

"Well—" She sputtered. "We haven't even met."

Luke stuck out his (very large) hand. "How do you do? I'm Luke Patterson. I'm a fireman." He grinned. "I'm a very nice boy." He didn't bother to mention the part about his impressive size because, hell, she could tell that for herself.

His palm skated across hers, and suddenly he didn't want to let go. Touching her was like coming home after a long, hard shift. Relaxing. Comfortable.

But not too comfortable. A sizzle ran up his arm.

"I'm Trish." She stared as though the feel of his skin, this indefinable *connection,* had her just as befuddled and bewildered.

"Ask her to go *out*," Mrs. Lipniki prodded. She had both eyes open now and watched avidly. "She's free on *Saturday*."

"Oh dear." A charming pink tide washed up Trish's cheeks.

She tried to tug away, but he still had hold of her. He wouldn't let her escape. No way. No how. Luke cleared his throat. "So," he said, "would you like to go to dinner? Say, Saturday?"

She gulped, drawing his attention to the long, slender column of her throat.

"Oh, go on, honey," their matchmaker crooned. "He's not an axe murderer."

Trish sputtered a laugh. When she noticed the intent look on his face, she sobered. "I would love to."

"Great," Luke said, but he doubted Trish heard him, because Mrs. Lipniki said it at exactly the same time, and a whole lot louder.

"Great!" she crowed. "He'll pick you up at six!"

Luke blinked. "I guess I'll...pick you up at six."

Trish laughed again, which sent shivers down his spine; he really liked the sound of it.

"So...you gonna be okay, Mrs. Lipniki?" Izzy asked.

"Oh, yes, young man. I think I'll be just fine." She winked in his direction.

As they made their way back to the truck, Izzy chuckled. "Another false alarm."

Luke didn't respond. He had hope. Maybe it would be the real thing after all. He wouldn't find out until Saturday.

He picked up Trish right on time, because he knew if he was late Mrs. Lipniki would have something to say about it. She usually had something to say about everything.

And yes, the old woman was on her stoop, waiting.

Luke nodded in greeting as he rang Trish's bell.

His date answered his summons as though she'd been waiting at the door. The sight of her stole his breath. She wore a slinky blue dress that clung to her curves and heels that made his mouth water.

He wanted nothing more than to get her someplace private where he could explore her body at length. With his lips. He didn't expect that would happen tonight. Mrs. Lipniki had said she was a *good* girl. Good girls didn't go home with random men on a first date.

Damn, Luke hated to wait. But wait he would.

He could tell Mrs. Lipniki was in the mood to chat, so he took Trish's elbow and stated, very firmly, that they had reservations and couldn't dawdle.

Trish shot him a relieved smile. Mrs. Lipniki's face screwed up in a scowl.

Luke helped Trish into the car, disciplining himself to keep his hands off her, but his palm itched to test the soft flesh of her hips, to skate over the curve of her ass. It took everything in him to resist.

He slid into the driver's seat next to her and fit the key in the ignition. "All set?"

She tipped her head and observed him solemnly through thick lashes. "You don't have to do this, you know."

Luke stilled. "Do what?"

"Take me out to dinner. You were railroaded into that invitation."

"Was I?"

She nodded. Her throat worked. "Of course you were. But I understand. Mrs. Lipniki can be rather adamant."

"No one bullies me into doing something I don't want to do." He softened his words with a wink.

She blew out a weedy, trembling laugh and gestured to her body. "I'm hardly a runway model. I know men prefer slender women."

Luke gaped at her. "Not all men, sweetheart. Some men don't like making love to a stick figure." Her eyes widened in surprise and then warmed, so he shifted to face her with his arm over the back of the seat "I have a confession to make."

"Yes?"

"I love curves on a woman. When I saw you, all I could think about was how much I wanted to...well, hold you." The intensity between them notched upward. He cleared his throat. "You're exactly the kind of woman I prefer."

"Really?" Shock limned her exquisite features. Then an impish hunger replaced it. "Well, in that case, I have a confession as well. No, wait. Two."

Holy hell. With that look and the way she dabbed at her lips with her tongue, he couldn't wait to hear them. "W-what?"

"Remember how Mrs. Lipniki said I was a good girl?"

"Yes." Anticipation slithered through him.

She glanced at him from beneath her lashes. Heat shot between them. "I'm not."

Holy hell. A bolt of lightning seared him. His cock shot up like a meerkat on the prairie. "You're not?"

She shook her head. He liked the way her hair danced over her shoulders. He wondered what it would feel like fisted in his fingers as he guided her head, her mouth warm and tight around his—

"No. In fact," she leaned closer, "the things I like to do might blow your mind."

Luke shifted as his trousers became tighter. His cock throbbed manically. How on earth was he going to make it through dinner? "And your other confession?"

She nibbled her lower lip. He fixated on the sight. "I have a...thing for firemen."

"A t-thing?"

"Yes."

Her hand eased over onto his thigh, high enough that her pinkie brushed his aching balls—the hint of a caress. He almost came.

"W-what kind of...thing?"

Trish opened her mouth but never got to answer, because just then, Mrs. Lipniki, who was still standing on her stoop watching them with an eagle eye, bellowed, "I thought you had a *reservation!*"

Without another word, Luke started the car and drove away. Though he was in a lust-sodden daze engendered by a dizzying warmth on his thigh, he somehow managed to find his way home.

Dinner could fucking wait.

Trish Olsen shivered in anticipation as Luke pulled into the driveway of a modest home in a nice neighborhood. She could hardly believe she was here. With him. That he *wanted* her. He cut the engine and took her hand from his thigh and held it. The breath caught in her throat when he turned to her.

God, he was gorgeous. The most handsome man she'd ever seen, with a long aquiline nose, high cheekbones and dreamy brown eyes. His sandy blond hair caught the dying glints of the sun. Tiny golden prickles of beard dusted the hard sharp line of his chin. His neck was thick and roped with muscle. And his body... She ached to discover the splendor beneath that prissy dress shirt.

But his expression was somber. "Are you sure you want to move this quickly?"

Quickly? She'd been watching him for months, her heart pounding in her throat each time his paramedic unit pulled up in the drive. She'd even begun hanging out with Mrs. Lipniki more and more often in the hopes she might get to meet him. Even had the occasional fantasy about starting a grease fire in her own kitchen.

The bald truth was, she didn't have a thing for firefighters. She had a thing for Luke Patterson.

He seemed to be as taken with her as she was with him. But still, she had to ask. "I'm sure about this. Are you?"

His response was to tug her close, to pull her into his arms and kiss her.

Rockets exploded in her head when his soft, warm lips brushed hers. His mouth was perfect, a dream, moving over hers in a velvet buss. He tasted wonderful, like liquid lust. His hand skated to her hips, her waist, crept up to just barely cup her breast.

He groaned, deep in his throat. "God, yes." And he deepened the kiss. He nudged his tongue past her lips, into her mouth. When she sucked him, just a tad, he shuddered and reared back. The look in his eyes seared her. "Maybe we should go inside."

Trish had to laugh as she imagined how they must appear to any random observers, rushing from the car, skittering up the sidewalk, dancing impatient jigs as he fumbled for the keys. But once they stepped inside, once the door was closed behind them and they were together, alone, all thoughts—the illusion that anyone else in the world existed—evaporated.

Luke didn't wait. He didn't invite her into the living room and offer her a drink or make idle uncomfortable chitchat. He backed her up against the door and pinned her there with his long, hard body. She felt him, every muscle, every breath, every heartbeat. His hard cock, pressing into her belly, throbbed.

If she'd ever had any doubts about her allure—like, ever—Luke wiped them away with that embrace. She knew he wanted her and desperately so.

She wanted him in the same way. It was a burning, aching hunger in her womb.

The kiss devolved into something feral. They ate at each other, sucking and licking and grinding their bodies together at every point they touched. She explored his magnificent form, testing the firm, rippling muscles, scraping at his skin, yanking madly at the clothing separating her from heaven.

He pulled back and ripped off his shirt—buttons flew. Then he yanked down the neckline of her dress. He was a little gentler with her favorite dress than he'd been with his shirt, but not much. To keep it from ending up in shreds, she shrugged it off.

And he froze.

He froze and stared at her. His eyes, wide and brown, studied every contour, every curve. She wore nothing but lace—a skimpy bra restraining her generous globes, and a flimsy pair of undies. He lifted a hand to her chest; it shook.

When he cupped her in his palm, he let out an agonized hiss. "Jesus."

He held her like she was a delicate piece of porcelain. His thumb nudged a nipple, and she moaned. Her body was on fire for his touch. Her pulse thrummed—in her throat, in her nipples, definitely in her clit. God, how she wanted him to touch her *there*.

A wet warmth seeped between her legs at the thought.

"You're so beautiful." He stroked her body reverently, tracing the curve of her waist and arching out over her hips. He measured the curve of her ass. "So soft."

He tested the weight of her breasts with both palms, then pressed them together and took in the view with avid fascination. He buried his face in the cleft he'd created and inhaled deeply. Shuddered. A low groan rumbled from him. All the while, he tormented her swollen nipples with his nails. Delicious sensation danced through her with each swipe.

Trish clutched at his head, nested her fingers in his hair, and scored his scalp. To have a man like Luke worship her like this was beyond delicious. It was divine.

She ached to worship him as well.

She was about to turn the tables—to push him back against the door and explore and lick and delight his body—when he knelt down. Her knees nearly gave out at the sight of this man crouched before her, his beautiful face at crotch level. He kissed her belly, his breath hot on her skin.

She shifted her legs apart and his chuckle rumbled through her. He looked up and captured her gaze, held it as his thumbs hooked into the tiny strap of her panties and drew them down.

When he broke the connection, it was to dip his head and nuzzle her slick, swollen lips. Trish cried out and threw back her head as he found her clit. It wasn't difficult for him—her nub was swollen and thick. It was so engorged it nudged out from her protective flesh like an impudent tongue.

Oh. God. And speaking of impudent tongues! When Luke licked her, when he swirled around her bud and lashed it, Trish nearly swooned. "Oh, please," she groaned, holding him in place with an insistent grip. "Yes. Yes."

He nestled deeper, lapping and nipping and—oh god!—sucking.

She came then, lunging and howling and thrashing against his mouth. He did not stop. Was not deterred. Even as she lost all control, even as she was swept away by a wash of unbearable bliss, he slipped two fingers up into her clasping cunt and played her. Like a harp.

He kept her orgasm going for longer than she could have ever imagined, stroking her and working her and rubbing that spot deep inside that clenched and quivered and thrilled to his touch.

When she could take no more, when she was absolutely, positively, utterly replete, she collapsed onto the floor beside him. And found herself nested in a pile of his mail.

They'd never even made it a foot from the door.

Luke burned as he held Trish, reveling in her gasps and moans as she desperately tried to recover her equilibrium.

It thrilled him that he'd made her come so completely, so

wildly. And she was a wild thing. A vixen in heat. He would give her a moment to recover, but not much longer. Because he was so close to the edge, it hurt.

He bided his time, stroking her and kissing away her tears and fantasizing about what they could do next. Almost all his ideas involved his cock.

Because it was near to bursting. Aching to be in her. Anywhere.

He thought about bending her over the back of the couch, what it would feel like to hold on to her lush ass as he pushed himself deep into her tight cunt. He thought about taking her into the kitchen and drizzling chocolate syrup all over his cock for her to lick off. He thought about taking her in the shower, rubbing thick lather all over her magnificent breasts until they were slippery and slick—and then holding them tight and easing himself between them. He even thought about lubing up her pucker and anchoring his grip in her fleshy globes as he inched in.

And as he thought, his impatience—and his cock—began to twitch. His fondling turned from soothing to arousing. Casual caresses became deliberate strokes. It wasn't long before his Rubenesque beauty was ready again.

When she pulled him down for a steamy sultry kiss, he knew it was time. He helped her to her feet and led her into the bedroom. He fully intended to tease and torment her, to make her come once more before fucking that hot little cunt of hers, but Trish had other ideas.

When they reached the bed, she unfastened his trousers and sat him down. Then she knelt between his legs. And he couldn't stop her. He couldn't move. Because she took hold of his cock and stroked him.

Breathtaking waves of pleasure rocked him. He closed his

eyes and reveled in it. When she traced the thick veins, drew a fingertip over the bulging head, he saw stars.

"God, Trish," he growled. And then the growl became a whimper, because she took him between her lips and sucked.

Warm. Wet. Velvet heaven. He clenched his fists in the covers to keep from bucking into her mouth, to keep from fucking her like a sex-crazed animal. And holy hell, she tormented him. She licked and nibbled at his aching staff, sucking him in and swirling her tongue. Then she took him deep—so deep he could feel the muscles of her throat massaging his head.

Her finger, her naughty little finger, toyed with the star of his ass. Sensation speared him.

He couldn't bear it. He couldn't hold out. He couldn't—

She stopped.

Agony roiled through him. His eyes flew open and found hers. She smiled. It was a sweet, innocent smile—so incongruous with what those lips had just been doing. But Trish was a hellcat. He'd known it all along.

And now she proved it.

Her finger in his ass wiggled, just a little. He shivered.

She licked her lips. "I want your cock inside me, Luke Patterson. And I want it now."

Holy fuck.

With no preamble, he grabbed her and tossed her onto the bed. She landed on her belly, and he didn't hesitate, couldn't even wait long enough to turn her over. He came up behind her, pulled her up on her knees, fisted his cock and shoved it in.

She wailed at the invasion, a low warbling groan, then shimmied her hips from side to side to ease his passage. With her movements, the tight muscles of her cunt undulated, opening and closing on the head of his rod like a hot mouth. He slid deeper and a harsh shudder took him.

She was so wet, so scalding hot, so fucking tight. Her ass was soft against his groin as he pushed in to the hilt. He loved it. Loved the feel of her pressing back into him. "God, yes," he groaned. He hunched over her and began to move. Each plunge was met with a delicious resistance, a tormenting dance as she clenched around him.

"More," she panted. "More."

He complied. He held her still, as he had in so many fantasies since yesterday, and plowed in and out of her. Each stroke sent delight skittering along his spine. He sped up. Fucked her harder. She cried out and thrust back into him with a growing fervor.

Heat rose, blew through him. Delirium danced in his head. Faster and harder and deeper. Like a frenzied beast, he sluiced in and out of her slick cunt. She quivered, quaked, mewled, and a hot rain showered his cock. As she came, her walls loosened, easing the way for a more frenetic ride.

The insistent slap of skin to skin echoed through the room, twined with the sounds of her gasps, his grunts. She tightened again—he could feel another orgasm building deep inside her. The sensation drove him wild, licked at his sanity, eroded his control.

That tingle, that deep, slow burn began at the base of his cock and rose. He tightened his grip on her ass and pounded harder. She cried out, whipped her hips from side to side. Begged, pleaded, cursed.

And then, it hit.

Together, they crested the wave, tumbled into the abyss, exploded.

Cum snarled from him in jet after jet of scorching pleasure. She moaned and clasped at him in great grasping gulps as he flooded her, saturated her, filled her up.

They collapsed in a tangle of limbs, both shaking, panting, trembling as bolt after bolt of ecstasy lashed them.

They lay there in each other's arms for a long while, spooned together. Luke reveled in the way she felt, so soft and warm against his body. He loved the weight of her breasts in his hands, the curve of her bottom as she nestled his cock, her scent. He could hold her forever, he thought.

This delightful reverie was interrupted by a loud rumble.

Trish laughed and put her palm to her belly. "Sorry."

He rolled her over and kissed her. "We kind of skipped dinner."

"We kind of skipped a lot of stuff."

He stilled. Hell. They had. A condom for one. "But...did you...like it?"

She riffled the hair on his chest. "Of course I liked it. I loved it. I meant we skipped the small talk and the awkwardness. All the stuff I hate."

Yeah. They had. It'd been awesome. Still... "A little small talk would be nice. I'd like to get to know you better." A lot better.

She considered this. "Hmm. Maybe over dinner?"

He tucked her closer, bit back a smile. "Are you asking me out on a date?"

"I guess I am." He loved the way her eyes crinkled at the corners when she grinned.

"Do you like hot stuff?"

She gestured between them. "Apparently."

He chuckled. It was pretty hot between them. "I know a place that has a kick-ass chili."

"Hot chili?"

"Five-alarm chili."

"As hot as you are?"

"Hotter."

She blew out a breath. Her bangs floated up. "Hotter than Luke Patterson? I'd have to see it to believe it."

"Taste it. You have to taste it to believe it."

She grinned. "Challenge accepted."

So for their first date—after a wild, wild ride—he took her to Station 12 and fed her Izzy's Five-Alarm Chili, glaring at any firefighter who so much as glanced her way. She was his, after all.

And then he took her back to his house and made love to her all night, trying all the things he'd been fantasizing about.

And the reality was better.

In the morning he took her home and lingered on her stoop, kissing her good-bye. He was loath to leave, but he had to go to work. He could rest easy in the knowledge that they'd made plans for that night. And the next night. And the night after.

Maybe forever.

Once she was inside and had closed the door, he fished his keys out of his pocket. A movement to his left caught his eye. Mrs. Lipniki. Peering out at him through the screen. He sketched her a cocky salute.

"Out all night, eh?" She grinned.

Luke blinked at the realization she had not yet put in her teeth.

"I guess that date went well."

"Yes, ma'am. It did." He puffed out his chest. He couldn't help it. "Looks like you'll have to turn all your matchmaking efforts on Izzy now."

"Young man," she said with a wink. "You can count on it."

Ah. Poor Izzy.

Somehow Luke just couldn't dredge up an ounce of sympathy.

RENEGADE

Brindle Chase

Of all the stupid things a rookie could do, Officer Kara Brown had blundered so badly, they'd have to make a new category just for her. In the barely there dress she'd picked for the undercover assignment, her choices had been limited. But no, she'd picked her cleavage to hide the wire.

Kara scooted across the cold concrete floor of the warehouse. Her back ached from slouching with her arms tied behind an iron water pipe. The maneuver gave some slack to the handcuffs—her handcuffs—binding her wrists. If she was going to die, she might as well be comfortable. She'd been too anxious to slap the cuffs on these goons to prove her worth, and she'd stashed a set in her purse. It hadn't occurred to her the first place they'd look would be her ample mocha breasts.

Duh, Kara.

Always jumping first, thinking last. This latest decision topped them all, and she was going to pay with her life. The possibility of being shot was only the beginning of her nightmare.

The way the five gangsters groped her flesh with their hungry gazes made death welcome. They were going to rape her and *then* cap her. It didn't take a rocket scientist to see the writing on the wall.

Kara fought the panic welling in her chest. She wouldn't cry. *Death before dishonor.* Frantic, she scanned her surroundings for a way to kill herself so at least she would die with dignity.

Carver, the leader, stood over a makeshift desk. He was the smart one and scared her most. Allegedly, he raped women before carving them beyond recognition with a fillet knife.

A chill trickled down her spine, and she closed her eyes. Desperately, she wished away the horrific visual.

Keep your wits.

She opened her eyes and focused on the other gangsters. KK Jones, a psychotic biker, just out on a truncated ten-year sentence for second-degree manslaughter. He was a mountain of a man with a beard to match.

Reggie Jefferson, aka "The Bling," was a capable gangster. His being alive and not in prison at age twenty-eight was almost a miracle. Criminals were dangerous with an ounce of brains.

And cops were dead without an ounce more of gray matter than their adversaries. Terror clawed at her throat. She shook her head and looked to the remaining thugs. The other two she didn't remember from the briefing. All that mattered was they carried 9mms and listened to Carver.

Even if her backup could find her, she'd be dead before they could mount a rescue. A SWAT team was her only chance. They would send *Renegade.* Sexy, hot, Sergeant Michael Delaney. He'd wade through these pukes, leave a wake of death and sweep her off her feet. If there were a God, he'd take her as his reward.

The thought warmed her and sent a spike of erotic pleasure straight to her core. Many times she'd fantasized about the walking, talking death machine and his stacks of muscle. His wavy dark hair, rugged Italian features and deep mesmerizing eyes had invaded her private fantasies far too often. But he didn't know she existed.

Some said his methods bordered on police brutality, yet he always got the bad guy and society was safer for it. Either way, he made her wet. Since day one at the precinct, she'd gone out of her way to get his attention. Kara had jumped at the chance for this assignment. Not only to prove herself, but also to put herself on his radar. What an epic fail.

"She ain't no cop, fool," Reggie argued. "Cops ain't got legs like that."

"Don't be an idiot. Only a cop is stupid enough to wear a wire on us," Carver countered and crossed his thick, tattooed arms across his massive chest.

"Yeah, but check that little black muff. Bare as a schoolgirl. Shit, cops don't shave. Not even lady cops."

Kara realized her dress was too short for her seated position and her womanly wares were on display. She'd lost her tiny, delicate thong in the scuffle when they'd taken her. It explained why they kept looking her way every five seconds. Shifting onto a hip, she crossed one leg over the other and blocked their view.

On cue, they turned and looked straight at her. Their gazes drifted to the hem of her flimsy dress, and her cheeks burned with rage. She wished they would kill her and be done with it.

"She's a fucking Fed, I tell ya."

"Whatever, she is—" Carver stopped in mid-sentence and tilted his head to one side.

Then she heard it. Sirens. A lot of them. Her heart pounded triple time. They would kill her before her brothers in blue could break in and take out all five gangsters, but now they wouldn't have time to rape her.

"Fuck. Cops," KK growled.

"No shit, Sherlock," Reggie said.

Carver glared at Kara. She met his menacing stare with all the courage she could summon.

His eyes said it all. He lifted a meaty hand, scrunched his tattooed fingers and tucked them into a fist. A sinister grin stretched across his bronze face.

Like the angel of death, he moved toward her. Panic welled up her throat, and she swallowed the lump suffocating her. Fear clawed at her with its icy tendrils and tore away her courage in strips. Tears formed along her eyelids, and she fought her quivering lip.

Bang! Bang, bang! Gunfire split the air.

The face of the unnamed thug to her left imploded. A spray of blood splashed across the floor. His body slammed into the brick wall with a sickening thud. The bad guys scrambled for cover, and Kara frantically searched the dense array of shelving scattered around the warehouse. Whoever was shooting at them had just saved her life.

Muzzle flashes flared through a haze of smoke, and then she saw him. Kara's heart resumed its rapid thumping. It was *Renegade*—no mistaking the massive frame, the muscular broad shoulders and thick thighs. Delaney was built like a tank.

Time slowed as she helplessly stared in horror. Gunfire blasted from every corner of the warehouse. Crates and shelves shattered, exploding under the impact of bullets zinging back and forth.

The deafening roar of pistol fire thundered as bullets tore through wooden boxes and cargo while the thugs tried to shoot her hero down. She lost sight of him and scrambled onto her knees. She ignored the pain the awkward position brought, but that was the least of her worries. She couldn't see Michael.

"Did we get h—" The remaining unnamed thug's question died on his tongue as Michael Delaney popped around a steel shelf unit and blasted a salvo through the goon.

"Fuck, fuck, fuck." KK ducked behind a metal desk and slid in a fresh clip.

Reggie rolled onto his side and shot wildly in Delaney's direction. The battle was out of control.

If she wanted to live, she had to pay attention and be ready for an opportunity to escape. The outlook was grim, but there was still a light. Renegade was tearing them apart.

Through the haze, Michael crouched behind a crate and ejected a clip. His steely eyes locked on hers from twenty yards away and seared her with a ravenous hunger. The unspoken passion stole her breath. He'd never looked at her like that before. Or was it her imagination? He was so savagely beautiful, desire dove straight down between her legs.

"You have the right to remain silent…" Michael said snidely, then jerked up and fired a blazing hail of death at the criminals.

"Fuck you, cop," KK shouted with a squeal at the end of his words as he ducked a shower of wood shards.

"No, thanks. Not my type," Michael yelled. His husky voice sounded like gravel.

"You want the bitch? Come get her, pig," Reggie taunted. The injured gangster patted his pockets.

Her gaze shifted to his gun. The clip was out and he was searching for a replacement.

"Yeah, come get her," Carver repeated, then whirled down, dodging several shots from Michael. He snarled, jumped back up and fired five rounds before his gun clicked empty. He dove back down and ejected the spent clip.

Carver waved frantically in the air and got Reggie's attention. Carver shook the empty clip at Reggie expectantly. Reggie responded by showing his own spent clip, disgust curling his lips.

Hope flooded her veins. KK was the only one left with ammunition.

"Delaney, two of them are out of ammo. Just the biker has bullets," she cried.

Carver whipped around, and if looks could kill, she'd be dead.

Her fate was still up in the air, but she flashed him a defiant grin.

"Fucking bitch!" Reggie covered his wound and crimson flowed between his fingers.

"Where is he?" KK shouted. Kara could feel the panic rising in the thug. "Fuck. Fucking where is he?"

A clatter near KK drew several shots. Michael rose over a crate to the left of KK's firing arc and shot two more rounds at the biker. And then three dull clicks. He was out.

Kara's heart sank.

KK turned and aimed.

Michael ducked.

KK jerked the trigger of his gun. Another click. Time sped up.

"Fuck!" KK dropped behind the steel desk, but she could see his shoulders wiggle about. He was looking for another clip. He had to be out. Because surely there was a God.

Or was there? Movement to her left caught her attention. Carver flashed a savage-looking fillet knife and unleashed the most sinister glare she'd ever had the misfortune of being on the wrong end of.

It was a gamble, but she had only one chance. "They're out of ammo," she shouted. "All of them."

Carver froze where he was. A whimper came from KK's hiding spot, and Reggie simply collapsed onto his back in defeat. The truth of her words was revealed by their reactions.

"Well now. Wasn't that fun?" Michael asked. He stood up and holstered his pistol. Kara knew he liked danger, but this was crazy. With three punks left, and Michael with the only bullets, there was no need for bravado.

But *Renegade* wasn't stupid. She'd read every declassified file on him. His methods were outrageous, scary and daring, but never dumb. Kara pushed up on her stiletto heels to gain some elevation.

Delaney's black BDUs were torn across one thigh. The frayed fabric was wet with blood. His uniform was stretched over his massive frame and armor with the sleeves rolled up, showing his thick forearms glistening with sweat. For a fleeting second, she imagined them pinning her legs wide.

With a gasp, she shook the image from her mind. All the ammo pouches on his belt were empty. He was out of rounds, too. The fear swarming around her spiked once more. It wasn't over yet.

"Looks like we got us a problem," Michael said with deadly irony.

"Fuck you, cop. She's wrong. I got a full clip. Show yourself," KK screeched.

Kara saw Michael's lips twitch, and then stretch into a grin.

KK didn't realize Michael was already in the open. The bluff was an utter failure.

"Bring it," Michael dared.

Carver glared in the direction of KK. She couldn't see the silent body language, but Carver lurched and stood. From her vantage point, clinging to the iron pipe, she saw KK and Reggie rise up, too.

In turn, Michael stared each criminal in the eye. If they weren't scared, they were idiots. Michael was a massive chunk of masculinity. Savage. Raw. Powerful. Death incarnate. The three gangsters flanked Michael who stood in an open area between shelves and crates. She'd never seen him in action, but a burst of heat swept through her in anticipation.

Michael twisted, his thick legs set wide in a defensive stance, and tracked all three of his opponents seemingly with peripheral vision.

The air crackled with an eerie, *someone's going to die*, intensity. A snick came from the right and Kara saw the gleam of a buck knife shimmer in the dim, flickering lamplight.

"Let's do this," Michael said. The echo of his icy voice rang flat, like the death he promised.

Carver slashed at Michael, but the veteran cop spun away, double-stepped forward and smashed his elbow on Reggie's wounded shoulder. A series of snaps announced the fracture of bone, followed by spurts of blood. Reggie staggered back in agony.

Michael didn't hesitate; he curled a leg back and shifted his weight. KK's meaty fist flew past his helmet. In a blur of motion, Michael dipped, swung a leg out and clipped the burly biker.

Carver slashed again and missed the agile SWAT leader. KK's overweight frame crashed into the concrete floor with a shuddering boom. Reggie stumbled back to his feet in time to receive another elbow to his injured shoulder.

Michael flung a fist at Carver. The gangster sidestepped, but then the legendary cop reversed direction. Forcefully, he hammered his steel-toed combat boot into the throat of the recovering KK. The biker staggered back.

Kara watched in morbid fascination. Michael was awesome to behold. Reggie lunged with an animalistic growl. His knife dug through the rolled-up sleeve on Michael's left arm. Renegade whipped his arm in a twist, deflecting the blade's lethal strike, but taking a minor gash for it.

Like a fighter in a kung fu movie, he spun, chopped a leg into the gut of Carver, and landed a solid fist to Reggie's rib cage. Kara cringed at the gruesome crunch of bones.

The stabbing, hacking, punching and kicking action came as flashes. Wound by wound, the three criminals were pulverized into submission.

Reggie lay at Michael's feet, gulping in wet, wheezing breaths and clutching his chest. Kara was sure the man's snapped ribs had pierced his lungs.

KK lay bent at an awkward angle across a demolished crate. A jagged, blood-soaked plank of wood pierced through his lower back and stood out from his abdomen. The biker's eyes stared unfocused off into space, frozen by death.

"You like cutting up women?" Michael snarled.

Kara shifted to see. She knew Delaney had won the fight. Of course he had, but now he was going to execute Carver. No judge. No jury.

"Delaney. No," Kara cried.

The four men he'd slain were fair game. They'd tried to kill him and they'd lost. But Carver was captured. He had to be taken to jail. Michael's reputation was mythical. Everyone knew he crossed the line. But it was all in the name of justice. Wasn't it?

Michael stood over the defeated gangster. The front of Carver's wife-beater crumpled in Michael's leather-gloved grasp. The other curled in a massive fist and stayed poised, cocked back and ready to deal death.

Michael turned, and his steel gray eyes leveled on Kara. She swallowed in fear laced with arousal. His fury was terrifying and beautiful. "What for? For justice? So the courts can let him off on a technicality? Or set him free because there isn't enough room in the prisons? This fucker is a plague on society."

He was right. She blinked and focused on him. His piercing eyes bored into her. She nodded. It was the wrong thing to do, but the world was a better place without the likes of the murderous gangster.

Carver hung limp in Delaney's grasp, beaten and bloodied worse than Kara had ever seen. And then Michael twitched. His fist came forward with a horrible meat-tenderizing squish. Kara closed her eyes and wished away the horrible scene.

A slap of carcass against concrete resounded and was followed by heavy footfalls. Her handcuffs went slack with a click, and she opened her eyes. Michael scooped her up off the ground like she weighed nothing and curled her to his massive chest.

She couldn't help the tears of rejoicing. Horror still assailed every nerve in her body, but she was safe. Adrenaline pumped like furnace blasts through her veins, and she collapsed against him, sobbing.

He held her in his arms and walked her out of the warehouse. She clung to him for dear life, not wanting to let go. Kara buried her face in his chest as the clamor of squad cars, officers and people all around her filled her ears.

Shame replaced the waning heat of adrenaline. There weren't adjectives powerful enough to describe how badly she had fucked up. She couldn't face her brothers.

"She all right?" Kara heard Jacobs ask, and she felt Michael bob his head.

Her legs dropped, and she balanced on the five-inch heels still amazingly strapped to her feet. She opened her eyes and blushed at the impassioned gaze Michael aimed on her. She'd never felt more like a rabbit caught by a lion than right then.

Michael snapped his gloves off and tossed them in the squad car. He yanked off his helmet and threw it in as well. Then he turned back and fixed her with another dark glare.

Kara fidgeted beneath his scathing stare and smoothed the folds of the tiny dress draped across her breasts.

A blur came from her right, and his hand snagged the back of her neck and tilted her head back. She gasped, staring at him as he scrutinized her.

"Are you hurt?"

She shook her head. Her wrists were sore, but she was otherwise unharmed. Michael's abrupt arrival had saved her from untold horrors.

"You sure?"

"Yes. I...I'm okay." The touch of his hand was hot on her skin and sent sparks of arousal straight between her legs.

His hand dropped from her jaw and gripped the front of her dress and pulled. A wave of heat flushed her cheeks. The dress barely covered anything, and she knew her breasts were in full view although his body shielded them from anyone else's sight. At his mercy, her sex clenched moistly.

"What fucking asshole dressed you in this?"

Kara looked down in shame. "I... I did."

"Seriously?" His voice was steel and electricity trickling down her spine.

She nodded. His damning gaze narrowed, and she swallowed hard. Kara knew he would never hurt her even though he was the deadliest man she knew.

"Yo, Delaney. Lieutenant wants to debrief Brown," came a voice from over her shoulder.

Michael nodded, but his stare remained on her. She looked to her open-toed shoes and focused there. Her toenail paint hadn't chipped through everything.

"I'll make sure she gets there, but me and her are gonna have a little chat about police work one-oh-one." His grave voice conjured another lump in her throat and forced her to swallow.

"Get in the car," he said with an ominously quiet tone.

"I know I screwed—"

Michael snared her wrist before she knew what happened. He spun her to face the open passenger door of the squad car and slapped her ass loudly. It stung but fueled her raging hormones as much as her outrage. Thinking he'd spanked her in front of half the precinct, she whirled in place. The flooding heat reversed from her core to her face. But his massive frame stood in the way and no one had seen. Relief washed through her. Of course he wouldn't humiliate her like that.

"Get in the fucking car." The edge in his voice brooked no argument. A darker part of her wanted to obey his every wish regardless. Michael Delaney had touched her butt. A grin tried to fight its way onto her face, but she shook it off.

She twisted on the towering heels and slid into the car. The door slammed against her shoulder, and she scooted into the seat.

Michael got in on the other side, slammed his door too and shoved the key in the ignition. Kara squirmed, trying to no avail to find a way to sit and allow the skimpy dress to cover her with some semblance of decency. The outfit simply couldn't comply, so she crossed her legs and stared at her knees.

He started the car, slammed it in gear and peeled out. Nineteen agonizing minutes of silence later, he slammed on the brakes. They skidded to a halt at a turnout on the side of the mountain road overlooking the city. The valley below was a field of lights as twilight surrendered to the night.

Michael threw open his door, rounded the front of the squad car and yanked open her door. He reached in before she finished undoing her safety belt. Grabbing her wrist, he pulled her from the car.

There was no chance to adjust her dress, and the summer breeze brushed across her hardening peaks. He spun her toward him and surveyed her savagely. Inch by inch, he inspected her and the intensity of his gaze melted her from within.

"Are you stupid?" he snapped.

"I... I thought—"

"What if I hadn't gotten to you?"

Stunned by his question, she met his hard gaze. What did he mean?

"Do you have any fucking idea what guys like that do to women like you?" He grabbed the front of her dress and yanked it up. He didn't seem to care her breast fell out as a result.

Excitement swelled through her, and her nipples tightened. "Wh... what?"

"Dammit, Kara."

Her heart fluttered at his gruff utterance of her name.

"Ever since you came into this precinct, I tried to ignore you. To not think about you... This..." He shook her barely there dress in emphasis.

His gaze blurred into hunger as it dropped, and she felt it sweep across her exposed flesh. "I..."

"You almost got your ass killed."

She stared. This wasn't a chewing out for being a stupid rookie. There was real heat, true passion in his words. Michael was upset. She knew she should make some effort to cover her breasts, but letting him see them was a thrill she had only imagined before today. "But I—"

"But nothing. If I hadn't been close by, you'd be dead. I can't have that."

"I'm sorry—"

His chest heaved with emotion, and his gaze slid up from her breasts to meet hers with hardened resolve. "I can't protect you like this, and I can't stop thinking about you. So... So you belong to me now."

Her pulse doubled and a wave of heat rushed through her.

"I...belong to you?"

"Yes."

"I..." Speechless, she stared back.

"Don't even pretend you don't feel it too. I've wanted you from the second I laid eyes on you, but I tried to ignore you. That ends now."

In emphasis, he tore what remained of her dress from her and left her mocha skin completely bare. Kara trembled beneath his heated stare, vulnerable and totally naked. His ravaging stare never left her as he tossed the remnants of the shredded dress into the car.

"You're mine, Kara."

His lips seized hers, and Kara moaned as he crushed her body against his, knowing what she'd tried to deny since the day she'd met him.

She did belong to him.

Completely.

Kara melted into his possessive kiss and yielded to his claim. In the hundreds of fantasies she'd had about Michael, nothing could have prepared her for the reality of his dominance. His greedy lips consumed her, and his tongue battered through to hers and flickered. Fire swept through her, and she thought she might faint.

His tough hands scooped her breasts, and he glided thumbs across her aching nipples. His touch was surprisingly gentle, but fierce all the same. In the middle of nowhere her wicked dreams of Renegade were going to be realized. Michael Delaney was going to fuck her, and she couldn't be happier.

He broke the kiss with a growl and bit her chin lightly. "You deserve better than this." Michael pushed her backward, and then turned her. "Better than out here."

Kara braced herself against the hood of the car and widened her stance. God, she needed him inside her.

"But baby, I need you." He swatted her ass with a stinging slap and grabbed it like he owned it.

Kara hissed at the spark of pleasure it sent straight to her core.

"I need to fuck you. Right here. Right now."

His words seared her flesh like lava, and her pussy clenched in excitement. It was crazy, wild, but the road was remote, and it was unlikely anyone would come along. She needed him to claim her, and the risk of being caught only made it hotter. They were long past the point of no return.

Kara looked over her shoulder and arched her back. If her eyes didn't say it, she was no longer too afraid to utter the words to him. "Take me."

Men like Michael Delaney afforded no indecision, and he lifted her ass up with one hand and yanked open his belt with the other.

Kara watched in lust-stricken anticipation as he pulled out his huge, thick cock.

He jerked her hips, bucked and impaled her slippery pussy in a forceful plunge.

Waves of hot pleasure rippled through her as she stretched to take him all. Kara whimpered in ecstasy. *Finally.*

Fast, hard and deep, Michael fucked her tightness and took her over the edge within minutes. Kara clung to the car for dear life as she came a second time, and Michael sealed his claim by pulling out and marking her ass with his cum.

He collapsed against her and held her tight. Together, they sucked in air until the orgasmic tremors faded. Turning her, he took her face into his strong hands and kissed her tenderly. He took off his uniform shirt and put it around her. It was longer than the skimpy dress she'd worn and draped just above her knees. She smiled in thanks and understood the gesture was more than offering her clothing.

"I have to get you back to the lieutenant," he said gruffly.

"Yeah..."

"Let him bitch you out. Don't argue. I'm putting in a request to have you transferred."

Kara was stunned. He'd fucked her, now he was sending her away?

"I can't have you getting into shit like that again. I can't be there to protect you, so I want you to transfer to SWAT training."

Stunned again, Kara stared in disbelief.

"I need you with me. Where I can protect you."

"I can protect myself—"

"I know." He traced a calloused fingertip across her lips. "I know you can, Kara. But that's my job now."

What could she say to that?

Michael slid his hands under her chin, lifted her onto her tiptoes and kissed her possessively. Amazed no one had driven by, they got back in the car and drove to headquarters. He stopped out front and took out a card. He wrote his address across the front and slipped it into her hand.

"Go, check in. Then get your ass to my place."

Kara couldn't wait; right now she grinned. Sometimes dreams did come true.

PAINTED

Leah Ridgewood

Bitter coffee burned Rosalia's tongue. The steaming black brew from her *abuelita's* corner store wasn't nearly as good as the stuff from the trendy café across the street, but she drank it as a matter of principle. The same principle, in fact, that demanded she scurry up to the third floor of rickety scaffolding at seven-thirty on a cold and foggy Thursday morning.

The thought of spending the day at the top of the scaffolding made her queasy, but she'd only rented the hulking atrocity for a week. So even if heights turned her into a trembling chihuahua, she had to get her skinny ass up there and finish the mural. It was her act of protest and her tribute to *abuelita*, and it already looked pretty damn good.

The three-story-high painting splashed turquoise, gold and magenta on the side of the building; *La Virgen's* white back-drop stood in bright contrast to the sooty wall. Rosalia had wanted to script giant letters advertising her family's *bodega*. But the landlord had told *abuelita* no. Rosalia's grandmother was sick and wasn't getting better. Once she died, the landlord would turn the storefront into a gourmet donut shop, or something equally stupid, catering to the new, wealthier residents of the neighborhood. Meanwhile, Rosalia would lose the rent-controlled apartment that went with the storefront.

Her hands balled at the thought of the landlord and his arrogant nephew who'd moved in upstairs. No doubt they thought the mural added a bit of local color and deterred graffiti. But in Rosalia's heart, *La Virgen* marked the building as part of the real Mission District.

She took her third sip of coffee and dumped the cup into a green sidewalk trash can. Hefting her knapsack, she readied herself to face her fear. Paint, brushes and turpentine weighed heavily on her shoulders. The rungs of the scaffolding were spaced so far apart she could barely keep her balance as she hauled herself up. At the top, she dragged her legs onto the planks and pushed onto her knees. The wind blew harder, threatening to topple her. Teetering precariously, she leaned into the gust. Her pulse swirled out of control, and the sidewalk spun beneath her.

She swung her pack down and sat. Squeezing her eyes closed, she leaned against the wall, her head resting against a window. A few deep breaths calmed her panic enough for her to notice the window leaked the sound of rhythmic keening— the nerve-grating sound of two beautiful jerks fucking—and enjoying it too.

It took no effort for Rosalia to imagine her handsome new neighbor and his girlfriend, limbs entangled, flawless fair skin and golden heads, big muscles and bigger breasts. It took even less effort for her own lean, brown body to slide into the image in place of the buxom blonde, her legs encircling his perfectly sculpted ass, his broad shoulders bunching and straining over her. Desire poured into her veins, erasing her panic and making her pant.

Hijo de puta. If they woke up *abuelita* with that caterwauling, she would raise hell and then complain to the landlord. Not that it would matter.

She shook her head, but the image of his gorgeous body gripped her. From the window of the apartment, she'd watched him come and go like he owned not only the building, but the world. His blond head towered above everyone else on the street. He didn't even have a job—came and went whenever—sometimes home all day, sometimes gone all night. Just another entitled pig stealing her neighborhood, one *bodega* at a time.

The resentment sobered her, and the last threads of her acrophobia unraveled, freeing her to work. She stood on stable-enough legs and pivoted, relieved to find the window heavily curtained. She didn't have to see what that fair skin over bulky muscle looked like under his fashionably ratty clothes. And, away from the glass, she couldn't hear them either.

She'd saved this high section of the painting for last—*La Virgen's* crown held aloft by tiny brown-skinned cherubs. With new purpose, she found a pencil and darkened the sketch she'd already made on the siding, adding detail to her little cherubs. Soon they would be chubby brown babies crowning *La Virgen,* their queen. But first, Rosalia layered bright-yellow paint onto the rays of light surrounding the holy mother.

When she finished tinting the array, she cleaned her brush, swooshing it around in the small jar of turpentine. A bit of the cloudy liquid sloshed out, and she peered over the side of the platform to see if it had splashed anyone. It hadn't, but a sleek, towheaded ponytail emerged from the door.

Without deliberating, Rosalia dropped the jar off the scaffolding. Well, perhaps she thought a bit—she did aim a good ten inches behind the blonde bitch. Which meant when Mr. Muscles appeared at the bottom step, filling out a navy-blue uniform like the sex-god he'd sounded like, the jar shattered at his feet.

He smelled paint thinner before he realized what had happened. The mural painter had dropped a jar from the scaffolding.

"What the hell?" shrieked Meegan.

He braced himself for her outrage. She hated coming to his neighborhood and never hesitated saying so.

She pointed at the painter. "Get down here this instant. I want an apology. And you barely missed my purse with that nasty stuff."

He followed the line of her finger to see the silhouette of a boy in a baseball cap and overalls.

"I said, get down here. Oh, for Christ's sake. Do you even speak English?"

The sole of his boot crunched in glass as he reached for Meegan's arm. "Are you hurt?"

"That's not the point. She'd have killed me, if that thing had hit my head. She probably did it on purpose." Meegan rummaged in her purse, shouting. "I'm going to call the police if you don't come down here."

He squinted up at the boy, a dark shape in contrast to the foggy white glare behind him. Had Meegan said *she*?

"Fuck you," said the painter, in an unexpectedly high voice. Yep, she.

Meegan stomped her foot. "Get down here."

"*Yo no recibo órdenes de gringas perra con palos por el culo.*"

He stifled a laugh. She'd pegged the bitchy and uptight Meegan, for sure. The laugh died in his throat. Why was he sleeping with her if that's what he thought? Little miss painter had shown him the light.

"What did she say?" Meegan asked.

He shielded his eyes and saw the mysterious woman had removed her cap. Sunlight fell on waves of raven black hair and a full-lipped, sensuous mouth, pulled into a sneer. She was easily twenty-five, but petite.

"She said it's a long way down, and she sees no need to descend."

The painter snorted. "That's not—wait. You speak Spanish?"

"*Sí.*" And he would use it to ask what had happened. "*¿Sabía usted lanza el frasco en ella?*"

"*Fue un accidente.*"

"An accident. You heard her, Meegan. Let's go."

"Not until she apologizes."

The painter let out a stream of curses in Spanish so fast and loud it made his head spin. He wouldn't fool Meegan about those, so he grabbed her, dragging her toward the train station.

The shouts cut off abruptly. "Hey. Why are you wearing that?"

He glanced over his shoulder, the light behind her illuminating the swell of small breasts and gently curving hips. They distracted him from her question, but he refocused. "What?"

"That uniform. Why are you wearing that?"

He shrugged. "For work."

"You work?"

From her tone, he may as well have said he was a Martian. "Uh, yeah. Paramedic at General," he called out, dragging Meegan behind him.

In the station, he shoved her onto the train with more force than he preferred to use with a lady. His sense of honor recoiled, even though she'd proven herself to be anything but. A clock over the turnstiles warned he was running late. His work boots and heavy pants weren't ideal for a run, but he jogged the eight blocks to the sprawling redbrick complex of San Francisco General Hospital. With a few minutes to spare, he powered up his phone and discovered five texts from Meegan, the last of which said, *Call back now or we r thru.*

Nice of her to make it easy on him; one of the nicer things she'd ever done.

A routine day of emergency calls followed—a heart attack, an overdose, a car accident, and in between, plenty of waiting. Sipping hospital coffee and burning time, he recalled the surprisingly beautiful mural painter's sneer. A tickling suspicion formed—it hadn't been an accident at all. He should be mad, but instead he admired the feisty little thing, and her judgment about Meegan had proven better than his own. If the painter was back in the morning, maybe he could get her number.

After his shift, he crossed the intersection toward his building. Lit by the bluish light of a streetlamp, the mural seemed nearly finished, though the scaffolding obscured it. He wanted to see it uncovered, and to see its painter even more. Hopefully tomorrow.

He closed the gate behind him, climbing the unlit stairs to the landing. A door opened. Once again in silhouette, she appeared in its frame. She closed the door behind her. As his eyes adjusted to the dark, her features came into focus. Glittering almond-shaped eyes seemed made for laughter, but they were narrowed. Under her slightly upturned nose, those full lips were pursed. Her dark hair spilled over her shoulders like shiny silk.

"You live with Mrs. Lopez?"

She didn't reply.

"The mural looks great."

She tried to skirt around him, but he wasn't ready for her to go. He blocked her.

"Let me past."

"No." Her eyes widened, and he cursed. What the hell was he thinking?

A big guy alone with a beautiful woman in a dark stairwell. He retreated.

Her chest rose with a deep breath, and she seemed more at ease. Instead of moving past him, she crossed her arms. "Where's your girlfriend?"

The scathing tone should have chilled him, but whatever hid behind the question made his body come alive, tightening his chest and stirring his cock. "Not my girlfriend anymore."

A husky laugh filled the stairwell. "Why?"

"I took your side."

"Did you?" She raked her fingers over her forehead and through her gorgeous hair.

"You know I did, and I suspect I was wrong. But I'm not sorry. Were you trying to hit her?"

"I was trying to hit you."

Her lie made him laugh. "What's your name?"

"Why do you care?"

"We're neighbors, and I owe you a thank-you for saving me from Meegan. Can I buy you a drink?"

Her throaty laugh rang out again. "We don't go to the same kind of bars. Go find another blondie."

"What's your problem?" He reached for her wrist.

She gasped, and a warning alarm went off in his head—don't push her. But she let him pull her close, her eyes huge and her breathing quick. He bent his head to her ear and spoke with a lungful of hot air against her neck. "Tell me your name."

"Rosalia." She leaned in, bringing their bodies into the barest contact. Some part of her liked him, behind all that resistance, and he was damn glad.

"I'm Justin." His chest burned where her breasts, small and firm, brushed against him. He wanted to reach under her blouse. "And if you won't let me buy you a drink, I'll have to kiss you instead—to show my thanks."

Not a word. No yes, or no. She simply tilted her face up and parted her lips. He intended to be gentle and slow, but her open mouth proved too tempting. His tongue delved inside, seeking out hers. He stroked the inside of her mouth, where the taste of something sweet lingered. She whimpered, and all he could think of was taking her to his bed. Except Meegan had been there last night, and the sheets needed changing.

He must have hesitated, because Rosalia pulled away.

"You're welcome." She slipped under his arm and down the step before he could stop her.

He followed, but the street was empty. At the corner, he looked in both directions. She'd vanished. Some primal instinct told him to chase. But no, she needed him to prove something to her. He would figure out what it was, prove it, and she would stop resisting. He went back upstairs to change his sheets.

Rosalia was not a burrito, or, for that matter, any other kind of local flavor for Mr. Muscles to sample at his convenience, which was why she walked away from that nearly all-consuming kiss. But at three A.M. she lay awake, tangled in her sheets, imagining him unwrapping and devouring her. That hot mouth, that big, forceful tongue—the memory kept her wanting and aching.

When she got out of bed, she drank a full cup of *abuelita's* toxic coffee. Then she steeled herself to climb right up the ladder and finish the cherubs. On the topmost platform, she lined up her jars of paint. The scaffolding swayed in the wind, and her hands shook even though she never looked down.

She dipped her brush into the chocolate-brown tint.

He wasn't a trust-fund jerk. He was a paramedic. He took her side against his girlfriend—ex—even though Rosalia had been in the wrong. And he was big and strong and on the other side of the window, in a room with a solid floor. Surely, with him pressed on top of her, the world would stop spinning.

Damn it. Her stomach churned around caffeinated acid, and her sleep-deprived brain took for granted that he wanted her. Last night it had sure seemed like—

The scaffolding creaked, its joints straining against the gales of another foggy morning. She couldn't breathe. The panic came from nowhere—or from fatigue and caffeine and being more than thirty feet over the sidewalk, and maybe from the realization she kind of liked Mr. Muscles. She trembled; the scaffolding quaked. *Dios mio*, it was going to fall. She scrambled to the ladder, knocking a jar of paint against the wall of the building. She froze with her feet dangling over the edge and her fingernails digging into the old planks. Her heart attempted to explode. She hiccuped, sobbed. She was going to die. Splat. Right on the sidewalk outside his window.

The very one now rattling and sliding open.

For one long moment her heart stopped pounding and she stared at him. Tousled hair and sleep-pink cheeks made him boyish. The muscles under his T-shirt did not. His eyebrows pulled together, then his eyes widened.

Oh right, she was in the middle of a panic attack, dangling from the scaffolding. Gasping, her legs flailed for purchase.

"Shit. Are you okay?" He rolled out of the window gracefully and gripped her wrists, hauling her back onto the platform.

She sucked in a breath. "Afraid of heights."

"What are you doing up here, then?"

She shrugged, hoping it hid her shakes.

His blue eyes almost matched *La Virgen's* dress, and when he smiled, they crinkled at the edges. "You're a stubborn little thing."

"Thanks for saving me." She couldn't look at his face, so she stared at his very broad chest.

"You weren't gonna fall." He reached for her wrists again, as if he didn't believe his own words. His big hands were warm and they steadied her pulse.

"I couldn't move. I freaked out."

He tugged her toward the window. "Come inside."

Anything was better than going back down the ladder. She followed. His room was sparse, like a bachelor had moved in three weeks ago, which he had. Her eyes strayed to the bed, and she remembered blondie's keening. A blush burned her cheeks, and of course he was watching.

He jumped onto the bed, boyish all over again, pumping his arms to bounce up and down on his knees. "She's gone. I changed the sheets and everything."

She almost smiled at his silliness. "Hey, I just came in to get off the scaffolding."

"If you say so."

Smug son of a bitch. She scanned for an exit and made a dash.

"Wait. Don't go—" Fast on his feet, he blocked her way, his big frame filling the doorway. "Why are you running?"

"Maybe I don't like you."

He cocked his head, making it clear he knew she was lying. "Why?"

"You're not my type."

He kept on staring like he could read her mind if he looked

hard enough. "You have a thing against blonds?"

Shaking her head, she giggled in spite of herself. In a way, maybe she did. And he made her giddy.

"Don't want Mrs. Lopez to know?"

Rosalia's giddiness deflated and tears stung her eyes. He'd found her sore spot—time to leave. She pushed past him. He grabbed her arm and yanked her back.

"Let me go."

"Stay."

She tried to twist free, raising her voice. "You're hurting me."

As if her skin were on fire, he dropped her elbow and took a step back. His eyes traveled over her, assessing whether she was truly injured. Satisfied she was intact, he asked, "Is she very sick?"

"*Si*." Rosalia wiped her eyes with the back of her hand.

He opened his arms, offering an embrace. "I'm sorry."

She waved him off.

Hands on hips, he studied her. "What are you afraid of?"

"Nothing." But, god, she wanted to tell him. Bad. She backed up onto his bed, scooted to the headboard, and circled her arms around her drawn-up knees.

"If she dies, will you lose the apartment?"

She nodded.

"Have you asked my uncle to add you to the lease?"

She let her head fall back, thudding the wall. "Why would he? He can get four times the rent."

"He's a good guy. Promise you'll ask."

"I don't want charity."

He blew out a long breath. "You're as stubborn as Meegan."

Real smooth talker. Tension spiraled up her spine and

launched her from the bed. She dashed outside, cascading down the steps two at a time and slipping into her apartment.

Abuelita lay in her bed, tucked under a colorful blanket. Footsteps creaked on the floorboard of the hallway. He'd followed her.

Like a sentry at the door, he kept watch while she smoothed *abuelita's* gun-metal gray hair and straightened the blanket. When she finished, he vacated the doorway and padded after her into the hall.

She pointed at the front door and hissed. "Get out." Spinning on the balls of her feet, she made for the cool white light illuminating her room at the end of the hall. She hurried inside, closing the door behind her. Or trying to. A very large foot prevented her from shutting it.

"Go away."

"No."

She gave up, sat on her bed and curled into the same knee-up defense she'd assumed upstairs. His eyes darted around, pausing on the window, shaded by the top tier of scaffolding outside. Then he scanned the well-used furniture. Her portraits—faces of her family and the neighborhood—hung on every wall.

"These are good." The appreciation on his face thrilled her, made her breaths come fast. Then it changed to something hard-edged, his jaw setting. "So, I'm not one of you? I don't belong...?"

She pointed her chin away from his laser stare.

He vaulted onto the bed and yanked her ankles out until she was horizontal. Pressing her into the mattress, he covered her mouth with his, silencing her protests. She wanted to shove him off, but underneath him she felt safer than she had in months, like her life wasn't disappearing around her.

He rocked her, thrusting his erection against her belly.

"What do you want?" he rasped in her ear.

To her horror, the answer poured out of her throat. "To not be afraid."

He pushed up, smiling. "Perfect."

His confident grin promised he could tame all her fears, and she wanted to believe it. Deftly, he unhitched her overalls. She lifted her hips and let him glide them off her legs. She fingered the hem of her sweater, which barely grazed the top of her panties.

"Keep it on. You'll need it." He lifted her like a bride.

She puzzled over his words until he sat her on the deep windowsill, smooth with a hundred layers of white semigloss. He shimmied open the half-stuck window. The second tier of scaffolding was almost flush with the sill. Before she could protest, he nudged her backward so that she lay on the rough planks, curtained by a flapping blue drop cloth. The street bustled underneath her. The iron frame creaked and groaned in the wind, and her panic gurgled in her belly.

Could anyone see her? Probably only glimpses.

Cotton caressed her legs as her panties came off in one swift move. His blond head lowered between her legs. A car horn sounded, jarring her. At the sweep of his tongue, she arched up, his mouth so hot compared to her already chilled skin. Blissful heat shot through her core and bloomed in her belly. But fear fluttered in her mind, attending to the sounds of the neighborhood.

"Rosalia, relax."

"If you want me to relax, put me back on the bed."

He chuckled. "Fair enough. Then focus, instead."

The rich tones of his voice anchored her. If only he would keep talking. But his lips and tongue went back to working miracles. He stroked her and licked her, teasing her with his fingers. Rough planks abraded her back through her sweater.

The scaffolding swayed; life went on below. Tension built in her pelvis, her hips rocking in time with the scaffolding and his tongue, a rhythm innate to her body and the universe.

He pulled back, breaking the sizzling contact. "I knew you'd be like this. Real." Then he sucked her clit into his mouth.

She bucked, her orgasm exploding through her with a single blast of pleasure. Her ears rang and her fingers went numb. In free fall, the wisp of her consciousness slid though the planks, down onto the street and into the earth—sinking, yet weightless.

Grasping her wrists, he pulled her to sitting and back into her body. He'd freed his penis from his pants—as big and hard as the rest of him.

"Condom?"

She shook her head. "Pill."

"Good enough. I'm safe." He pushed into her still-quivering core. Filled almost to the point of pain, she gasped then eased around him.

He grunted. Pinning her hips to the windowsill, he retreated, thrust again. Salty and smelling of her, his lips found hers.

His tender kiss trailed over her cheekbone to her ear. "No more fear. You'll stay. I'll take care of it."

The most mulish part of her protested. She didn't need his help, didn't want his protection. Pushing against his chest, she leaned back, and studied those azure eyes. On their glimmering surface, she saw what he really offered—affection, friendship, the possibility of something more.

With impressive patience, he waited, his erection pulsing inside her.

And suddenly it was true. She was no longer afraid. "Yes."

"Thank god," he rasped, then lunged into her with a frenzied rhythm born of too much restraint.

The sheer force of him inside her promised everything she needed. She lay back onto the platform, dug her heels into the windowsill and lifted her hips to receive him. With their gazes locked and their bodies moving in time, the neighborhood swirled around her and *La Virgen* looked down in approval.

When he came with a shout, Rosalia laughed—weightless and free.

BESIEGED

Elle James

Maxwell O'Brien pushed through the secret panel hidden in the closet of his bedroom in the embassy apartment he'd been assigned. Still wearing his dress mess from the dinner party he'd left moments before, he was careful not to brush against the dusty walls of the passage or the cobwebs dangling from the ceilings and corners of the doorways.

His heart raced as if he'd run through the streets of Kabul. Only he wasn't afraid of being shot at so much as being shot down by the ultimate disappointment.

Tonight he planned to ask Kate Seward, daughter of the U.S. Ambassador Extraordinary and Plenipotentiary of the small nation of Trejikistan, to marry him and follow him to his next duty station in Italy.

He'd discovered the passageway during his initial week exploring the embassy quarters located in an older, historic district of the capital of Trejikistan. A breakaway country from the Soviet Union, Trejikistan had seen a few years of peace, interspersed with the occasional secular strife and violence. At some time in the past, a former ambassador had been foresighted enough to design and construct several hidden passages known only to the ambassador and his most trusted staff members for use when a silent retreat was called for.

One such passage just happened to be located behind the ambassador's wing of apartments, including the one assigned to him. Max had been given a suite designated for family of the ambassador. Since Ambassador Seward's wife was deceased and he had only one child, he'd offered the suite to Max upon his arrival, claiming he wanted his bodyguard close by to protect his daughter.

Had Max known that Seward's daughter was a grown woman and one of the kindest, most caring and beautiful Max had ever known, he might have asked to be placed farther away to keep his distance physically as well as mentally.

From the first day, Kate Seward had been a force Max had to reckon with. Their mutual attraction had launched a game of cat and mouse Max ultimately lost when he realized he'd fallen in love with the confounded woman.

Now, he slipped through the passage connecting his room to hers, like he had on numerous occasions, praying the reflection of love in her eyes wasn't just a dream. She'd asked him to stop by and check the security of her room after the dinner party.

It was code for a lot more than checking security.

As he neared the panel that would open into her huge walk-in closet, his groin tightened, and he imaged Kate in that simple black dress she'd worn for the dinner party, her long dark hair pulled up in a sexy twist, wearing the pendant he'd given her for her birthday.

Max had sat near the end of the table, resisting the urge to tug at the tight collar of his dress mess uniform. If not for

Kate, he'd have begged to redeploy to the strife-ridden country of Chad—more comfortable in ACUs and face camo, training Chadian soldiers on antiterrorism techniques, than sitting at formal dinner tables.

He pushed aside the panel leading into Kate's room and stepped through, the ring in his breast pocket burning a hole through to his heart. He loved Kate, and he wanted her to be a part of the rest of his life. He'd planned on laying out clues for her to find over the next few weeks until finally he'd take her out to dinner and propose to her.

But today, he'd received his transfer orders. Max knew he couldn't wait, and he couldn't walk away from Kate. He didn't want this fantasy to end. Tonight, he'd ask her to marry him, and he prayed she'd accept.

When he stepped out of her closet into the bedchamber, at first he didn't see her. "Kate?"

"It took you long enough," she said, her voice low and sexy. She lay in her bed, the cream-colored sheets pulled only up to her waist, her breasts bare and tempting in the light from a softly glowing lamp on the nightstand.

Max stepped forward. "I hope you were expecting me."

"Only you, babe. Only you." She threw back the sheet and quirked her head. "Join me?"

His heart flipped in his chest, and his blood pounded through his veins as he ripped through the buttons on his uniform.

For such a proper ambassador's daughter, she was mind-blowingly passionate, a fact that still amazed him and made him burn with desire.

Max shrugged out of his jacket, hanging it on the bedpost.

"Let me help, or we'll be all night." Kate leaned up on her knees and reached for the buttons on his shirt, flicking through them with quiet efficiency. Then she tugged the tails out of his trousers and pushed the edges over his shoulders, her hands sliding down the muscles of his shoulders and arms. She pressed her lips to his chest, finding and nipping at the little brown nipple over his heart.

Max sucked in a breath and concentrated on control. He unbuckled his belt and slipped the hook free on his trousers, his motions jerky in his haste.

"Uh-uh." Her fingers caught his as he reached for the zipper. "Mine." Kate dragged the zipper down. "Always in uniform? Right down to the tighty-whities." She clucked her tongue even as she hooked her thumbs on the waistband of his trousers and underwear and pushed them downward until his cock sprang free. "Come to me." She stroked him, those supple digits sliding over his engorged shaft, her right hand reaching low to cup his balls and roll them between her fingers.

Patience shattered. Max kicked off his dress shoes and trousers. He grasped Kate's shoulders and lowered her to her back in the bed, then climbed over her. "You take my breath away."

"I try." She smiled up at him, her full, pink lips puckering. "Aren't you going to kiss me hello?"

"I'm going to do more than that." He nudged her knees apart and slid in between her thighs. "But first...I'll launch my own assault."

"Oh, should I be wearing camouflage...?" Her calf slid up the back of his leg. "And should I be carrying a weapon?"

"Babe, your *are* the weapon. You've completely pierced my heart and laid it open."

"Such sweet talk from a grunt." She wrapped her hands around his neck and drew him down to her. "Shut up and kiss me."

He lowered, his mouth claiming hers in a devouring kiss. He braced himself in the front-leaning-rest position so as not to crush her with his weight, the muscles in his arms tight.

When he came up for air, he forced himself to concentrate on pleasing her. If she let him, he'd spend a lifetime showing her how much he loved her.

Max started by laying siege to her throat, tracing a path from her chin to the base of her neck and tonguing the spot where her racing pulse beat crazily beneath the skin.

"I thought the dinner would last forever," she admitted, her hands skimming over his shoulders and down to his waist.

"I couldn't take my eyes off you." Max continued his attack, firing kisses and nips over her collarbone and the swell of one breast. He captured her nipple, sinking his teeth in, sucking in a strong hold on the defenseless treat.

Her back arched off the mattress in her surrender to his campaign of lusty torture as he moved down the smooth contours of her rib cage, across the field of taut abs to his ultimate target.

Max slipped his fingers between her folds and flicked the bundle of nerves—a move that never ceased to set her off.

Kate buried her heels in the mattress, her hips rising. "Please, Captain, I surrender. Take me."

He chuckled. "Not yet. You really should put up a little of a defense."

"How can I when you do—"

He tongued her clit.

"That!" she cried, her fingers clutching at his ears, pulling him closer. "Oh, please."

He pressed a finger into her channel and swirled it around. "Please what?"

"Do it again, damn it."

"Tsk, tsk. Such language from a diplomat's daughter."

"Just fuck me, soldier. Now." She tugged his ears.

"Careful. I might need those." He resisted, not done with her clit, tonguing her until she moaned.

Her hands fell to her sides, clutching the sheets, and her body stiffened. "I think I will die."

"No way. I've captured you; you're now my prisoner."

"I wouldn't have it any other way, unless it was with you inside me now," she said in a rush of words, her breathing erratic, her face flushed.

Max climbed up her body and pressed his cock to her entrance. "I love you, Kate."

"If you love me, take me." She grabbed his ass and slammed him home. "Oh god, yes."

Not exactly the response to his declaration he'd hoped for. He'd wanted her to say she loved him too. But too overwhelmed at that point by all the sensations ripping through his body, he let her comment slide into the deep haze of pleasure she always brought him.

Max thrust again and again.

Kate raised herself, matching him stroke for stroke, her fingernails digging into his buttocks.

All his nerve endings, all the blood flowing through his system seemed to center on the one place, that one moment when he shot over the top. One last thrust and he held steady, buried deep inside her. His breath caught and held. At the last moment, he jerked free, his come shooting out over her belly. When he finally dropped down beside her and pulled her into his arms, she snuggled close, her head on his arm, her fingers threading through the hairs on his chest.

Kate sighed, her eyes drifting closed. "You're amazing, soldier."

"Only because you make me that way."

"Uh-huh." She lay with her eyes closed, her fingers swirling softly against him.

He drew in a breath, ready to pitch his plea. "Kate?"

She didn't respond.

He leaned back and stared down at her. Her breathing had leveled, her breasts rising and falling in the slow, easy rhythm of one fast asleep.

Damn. Now he'd have to wait until morning. He pulled the sheet up over them and held her for a long time before he drifted off to sleep. In the back of his mind, he worried that she hadn't responded to his declaration of love with one of her own. Ah well, there was always tomorrow.

"Kate?" Max shook her awake early the next morning. "I have to get to work."

Her blue eyes blinked open. "So soon?" Her silky dark hair fanned out against the cream-colored pillowcase, the sheet slipping down below her breasts. "I can't convince you to stay a little longer?" Her hand slipped beneath the covers and swept across his morning hard-on. "Hate to waste...a moment with you."

"Your maid will be here any minute."

"That's all it will take." She rose to a sitting position, planted her hands on his chest and pushed him back against the mattress.

He tucked a strand of her hair behind her ear. "I had something I wanted to say last night."

"So, why didn't you?" She kissed his neck, her body shifting across his, her mouth trailing down to one of his taut brown nipples. "Can it wait until after?"

He caught her shoulders. "Damn it, woman, I have something to say."

As her teeth sank into the nipple, her hand slipped lower to capture his cock.

Thoughts of the ring still tucked in his jacket flew from his mind as her supple fingers tightened around him.

A surge of heat washed over his body, pooling low in his loins.

In the predawn hours of the morning, Kate slipped down his body, the sheets falling to the floor, her hands working magic against his skin.

Max closed his eyes as Kate pressed a kiss to the tip of his dick, the first taste of what was to come next from her hands and mouth.

His breath caught as her tongue snaked out to trace a circle around the rim, then slid down his length. A groan rose up his throat, and his fingers laced through her hair, holding her there.

Kate wrapped her lips around his cock. Her hand cupped his balls.

Max thrust upward, the head of his dick bumping against the back of her throat.

After several thrusts, he couldn't hold back. He pushed her back and flipped her over. Her legs fell open, her damp pussy glistening in the soft glow of a nightlight.

Max didn't pause long, thrusting into her, burying himself deep. Moving slower, he drew out to the very tip, savoring the slick heat of her channel.

When he hesitated at her entrance, Kate's hands curled around his hips, her nails digging into his flesh as she dragged him back inside her.

He settled into a fast and furious rhythm, rocking the bedsprings until they squeaked.

Kate's head tipped backward, a soft moan escaping her lush, pink lips. She planted her heels into the mattress and rose to take each of his thrusts, her breathing ragged, her body covered in a light sheen of sweat.

As Max catapulted over the edge, he yanked free of her channel, his seed spilling out across her belly. He rolled to her side and lay on his back for several seconds until he had his breathing under control. "You're incredible. And we forgot a goddamn condom again."

She turned to face him, a smile spreading across her lips. "You're not so bad yourself, Captain Delaney. And the condom is overkill. You know I'm protected." Her fingers threaded through the hair on his chest.

He grasped her wrist and held it away, forcing a frown when he wanted to grin. "There's something missing here."

Kate's brows puckered. "What are you talking about?"

Max sat up and reached for his dress mess jacket, hanging where he'd left it on the bedpost the night before. He fumbled to retrieve the single-carat diamond ring from the inside pocket, curling it into his palm before she could see.

Her eyes widened and her hand rose to press against her breast. "A present? But it's not my birthday."

Max's stern expression softened. "I wanted to do this last night, but you make it hard for me to think straight when you're lying naked in bed." He pulled her to a sitting position and captured her hands in his. "I'm a soldier, I like to keeps things simple."

"I wouldn't want it any other way." She batted her eyes, that sexy smile lifting the corner of her lips, making Max's heart race.

He pressed a finger to her lips. "Shhh. Let me get this right."

She kissed his finger and waited.

"I've got orders. I'm transferring to Italy."

"Oh, please no." Her brows wrinkled. "When?"

"In three weeks."

Tears filled her eyes. "Well, damn."

"Let me finish."

Her fingers curled around his.

"I don't want to leave..." he held up the ring, "without you."

Her eyes widened and the tears tipped over the edge and ran down her cheeks.

"Kate Seward, I love you. Will you marry me?" He held out the ring.

Kate shoved her finger through and cried, "Yes!" Then she flung her arms around his neck.

Max kissed her long and hard, holding the woman of his dreams in his arms, thanking God for bringing them together.

A knock on Kate's door forced him back to reality.

"Miss Seward?"

Kate pulled the duvet up over Max and covered her naked breasts. "Yes."

Max lay perfectly still.

The door creaked open and a woman's face peered around. "Your father is on his way to your room. Do you need help getting dressed?"

"No, thank you," Kate answered in a calm voice. "Could you bring me a cup of tea?"

"Yes, ma'am."

As soon as the door creaked closed, Max leaped out of bed. "I want to ask your father for your hand, just not like this."

"Tonight. I don't believe we have any dinners planned."

"I'll do that." Max slipped into his pants, grabbed his dress shirt and shrugged into his dress mess jacket. He jammed his feet into his shoes and crossed to the closet, pausing with one hand on the knob. With the other, he blew a kiss. "See you later."

Max slipped into the hidden passage and hurried to his room.

Since it was early, he changed into his PT uniform and tennis shoes and ducked out the gate of the embassy compound. His heart still pounded against his ribs and he had energy to burn.

Kate had said yes. Joy filled every fiber of his being, and he wanted to shout to the rooftops. Instead, he ran through the streets of Trejikistan, the steady beat of his feet hitting the pavement bringing him back into focus.

Four miles out from the embassy, he turned, ready to get back to see Kate, to hold her in his arms again, anxious to hear the words she'd yet to say. *I love you.*

As he neared the compound, the streets grew more crowded with young men, heading in the same direction as he was.

More than one jostled him, bumping into his shoulders and shouting at him in Trejik, their native form of Arabic.

With his short, military haircut and gray Army T-shirt, Max looked exactly like what he was, an American soldier. Apparently the crowd making its way toward the embassy wasn't pro-American.

Max ducked to the side, down an alley. Three dark-haired, dark-skinned Trejikistani's followed him, waving their fists and cursing him in their language. Two wore baseball hats, and one carried a tire iron.

At the end of the alley, Max turned. Into a dead-end alley. With nowhere to go and his back against a concrete wall, he'd make his stand.

He spun, braced his feet and waited, unarmed, undaunted. Three against one might scare most men, but not Max. He was Special Forces, a trained war machine.

The three assailants skidded around the corner and came to a halt, wicked grins spreading across their faces. With a wild whoop, the man with the tire iron rushed at Max.

Max dodged the tire iron, grabbed the man's arm and

yanked him hard, throwing him to his rear where the man's head slammed into the concrete wall. He fell to the ground and didn't move.

One down.

Max waved the other two forward. "Come on."

Incensed by their friend's treatment, the two remaining men launched themselves at Max.

Max slammed his palm up into one man's nose and threw a sidekick at the other man's shin.

Both men dropped to their knees.

Determined to end the fight there, Max kicked first one, then the other in the head.

Both crumpled to the ground and didn't move again.

Knowing he wouldn't last two seconds on the street in his PT uniform with an angry, anti-American mob forming, Max pulled the trousers off the man with the least blood and closest in size to him and dressed. He yanked his T-shirt off and replaced it with one with Arabic writing on it. Max slipped the baseball hat on his head, pulling it down over his forehead. He grabbed the tire iron and ran back the way he'd come.

Out on the street, he blended in with the mob moving toward the embassy. He kept his head down. Though he had brown hair, brown eyes and a tan from being outdoors, the color of his skin wasn't the natural dark tone of a Trejikistani.

Thankfully, the mob didn't notice, pressing forward and through the gaping gates of the compound.

Alarmed at the ease of their entry, Max paused at the gatehouse where both Trejikistani security forces and the Marine Corps Security Guards normally stood watch. One marine, dressed in his khaki shirt and royal-blue pants, lay in a pool of blood, unmoving.

Max's heart skipped several beats, and he raced for the back of the huge embassy building. Separate from the embassy, this structure housed the heating and air-conditioning units for the entire compound. From the basement of that utility building another secret passage led into the embassy. Max prayed that Kate, the ambassador and his staff had found the passage and were hiding in the relative safety of the basement until the Trejikistani military restored order among the protestors, or the American forces could arrange a rescue.

While the rest of the mob beat against the solid-steel front doors of the embassy and threw rocks and bricks through the bars covering the lower level windows, Max ducked around to the back, dodging another mob of people trying to go through the back entrance.

One rioter had a bottle filled with liquid and stuffed with a rag he lit with his cigarette lighter. Max's body stiffened. If the embassy caught fire, those left inside wouldn't stand a chance. If they didn't die from the fire itself, they wouldn't escape smoke inhalation. And as crazed as the mob was, embassy personnel wouldn't last long outside.

Fear for Kate and the other staff members sped Max's steps. He rounded the back of the utility building and edged through a bush, conveniently placed to hide a back entrance.

He wedged the tire iron between the door and the frame and forced the lock to give. It took several attempts before the frame bent, the lock gave, and the door opened outward.

Max rushed down the stairwell to the basement level.

When he hit the last step, the barrels of two M27 Infantry Automatic Rifles slammed into his chest.

Max's hands shot up and he whipped his hat off his head. "It's me, Captain Maxwell O'Brien, Army Special Forces."

The marine poked him in the chest again. "Why the fuck are you wearing that shirt?"

"I was out jogging and got caught up in the crowd. I had to blend in." Max dropped his hands and pushed past the marines. "Where's the ambassador and his daughter?"

"We haven't seen either one since Seward told us to get the staff to the safe house."

At that moment, two marines emerged from behind a large air-conditioning unit, the ambassador's arms draped over their shoulders.

"My daughter." Seward raised his head and coughed, his eyes red, his face blackened. "You have to get her out."

"Where is she?" Max helped the ambassador to the floor.

The ambassador shook his head. "She said she had to go back to get something important."

One of the marines stepped forward. "She took off before we could catch her and ran back toward her quarters."

"The hallways are filling with smoke," a third marine came out of the hidden passage, his face black with soot. "I didn't see Miss Seward. Hell, I could barely see my hand in front of my face. It's suicide to go back."

"We have to try." The marines handed off Ambassador Seward and turned to go back.

"I'm going. I know where she might be." Max pushed past them, ripped his T-shirt off and tied it around his face.

One of the marines who'd challenged him at the entrance grabbed his arm. "You might need these." He shoved his flashlight into Max's hand and a M9 pistol. "Semper fi."

Two marines followed, tugging their shirts up over their noses.

Max raced through the passage, the smoke having barely found its way to the lower levels of the hidden escape route. When he came to the passage the ambassador and the marines would have taken, he turned left instead of right.

"That's not the way," a marine called after him.

"Trust me." The corridor he'd chosen ended in a storage room stacked with large crates. "Help me." Max leaned his weight into a large wooden crate at the far side of the room.

The marines put their shoulders to it and the crate shifted three feet, exposing a concrete wall with a metal panel in the middle. Max dug his fingers into the side of the panel and pulled it open. He didn't hesitate, ducking into the long narrow hallway with stairs at the end. Not until he climbed the steps leading up to the second floor where the Ambassador's quarters were did the smoke begin to bother him.

Once in familiar territory, he didn't slow, racing past the door panel at the Ambassador's room to the one beyond it.

"Check that entrance and the next one past here," he shouted over his shoulder at the marines. "She might be hiding in there." Max flung open the small door inside Kate's closet. Smoke filtered through the closed closet door on the other side. Electricity to the building had been cut off and no light filtered through from the room beyond.

Max pushed through to the bedroom. The smoke hit him like a wall and he dropped to a crouch, his eyes stinging, his throat tightening. He fought to keep from coughing and alerting the aggressors to his presence. "Kate," he said loud enough so she could hear if she was still in the room.

Pounding footsteps sounded in the hallway followed by shouts in Arabic warning the marauders to get out before they were consumed in flames. Max shut off his flashlight.

As the footsteps retreated, Max hit the on switch and swept the beam around the room. The bed they'd shared earlier was empty, the sheets still disturbed. He checked beneath the bed. Nothing. "Kate."

The bedroom door burst open and a man wearing a T-shirt

around his head brandished an AK47 rifle and a flashlight.

Too late to turn off his own light and hide, Max rolled to the side and brought his pistol up as the terrorist aimed his AK47.

Max pulled the trigger.

His attacker's shot flew wide, and he slammed back against the wall of the bedroom, sliding down, eyes wide and vacant.

With the smoke thickening and no indication from the other marines that they'd found Kate, Max retreated to the closet, sure the shots fired would alert other rioters. He closed the closet doors behind him and whispered, "Kate, I hope the hell you got out."

"Max?" A soft voice sounded from deep in the shadows.

Max turned his flashlight toward what looked like a pile of clothing on the floor.

The clothing moved and Kate's dark head surfaced. "Oh, Max. I knew you'd come."

"Why the hell didn't you get out with the others?" He bent and scooped her into his arms.

"The power went out and I couldn't see."

He didn't waste his breath on more words. Instead, he picked her up and shoved her through the small doorway into the hidden hallway. Once on the other side, he closed the panel to limit the amount of smoke filtering into their escape route. The other marines emerged from their doorways.

"Got her." Max kept his voice low to avoid detection. "Can you walk?"

She held a scarf to her mouth and coughed into it before answering. "Yes."

He grabbed her hand and led her down the stairs and through the maze to escape into the utility building.

Kate ran to her father and flung her arms around him. "Oh, Daddy, you made it."

"Why did you go back? You scared years off my life." He patted her back, the lines in his face more pronounced.

"I had to," she said. "I'd left it on the counter."

"Nothing is as important as your life," her father said.

She smiled at him and held out her left hand. "I left my engagement ring on the bathroom counter. I had to go back and get it."

Max shook his head. "Damned female thinking. I'd have gotten you another." .

"But I love this one." She stood, her face smudged in soot, her hair in wild disarray and tears slipping down her cheeks.

"Is there something you two haven't told me?" Ambassador Seward pushed to his feet. A marine steadied him.

"Sir," Max stood at attention. "I'd intended to perform the formalities this evening at dinner."

"But things have changed." The ambassador waved his hand. "Get on with it."

All the staff and the uniformed soldiers and marines focused on Max.

He swallowed hard. "I would like your permission to marry your daughter."

The ambassador's eyes narrowed, and he seemed to consider it for a moment. Then he turned to his daughter. "And what do you have to say about this?"

"Daddy," Kate rested a hand on her father's arm. "I love him."

Max's heart sang at Kate's words. She'd never said them aloud, and to hear her declaration in a room full of trapped and desperate people who might or might not make it out alive, made it all the more meaningful.

Her father covered her hand with his, and then glanced at Max. "Captain O'Brien, given your loyalty and bravery, I couldn't think of anyone I'd rather have as a son-in-law. You have my permission."

A quiet cheer went up from the surrounding audience.

Kate stepped into Max's arms. "See? That wasn't so hard."

"Now we just have to live to the wedding day." He brushed the hair back from her face.

She smiled up at him. "We will."

Shouts outside the building drew their attention. The main exterior door opened and footsteps pounded down the stairs.

Max shoved Kate behind him and, along with every armed marine and Trejikistani security guard there, leveled his weapon at the stairwell.

The first man down the staircase was covered in desert camouflage from head to toe and sported an automatic rifle. When he saw the weapons pointed at him, he didn't back down, didn't raise his hands, but shouted. "Navy SEAL, Corporal Bryan Larson, reporting. Who's in charge?"

Max chuckled and lowered his weapon. "Kate, sweetheart, the cavalry has arrived."

"Navy SEALs, sir," the young corporal retorted. "Cavalry would be the Army."

PUMPING IRON

Christine d'Abo

Lila adjusted her sports bra, unfolding the doubled-over band, and hoped she wasn't about to make a huge mistake. Her recovery had been a long hard road, one she'd had to fight through inch by inch to be able to reclaim her body. But she'd made it and now stood on the other side, not simply back to her old self, but even better than before.

She only had one challenge left to conquer—Kyle.

Images of him kicking the asses of other UFC fighters were still fresh in her mind. She'd been intimidated as hell when she'd discovered he was going to be her trainer, having watched him beat and bloody men in the cage both on closed-circuit TV and at the gym. Kyle was vicious when he stepped in front of his opponent; any compassion he might have evaporated as the door locked.

Even in retirement he wasn't soft or compassionate when it came to training. He didn't give a shit about how much she hurt and kept pushing her to do things right. *Harder, faster, more, goddammit!* After a few sessions, she stopped being intimidated and really started hating him for making her work so fucking hard. It was a damn good thing her rehab was over and her body was in such good shape, otherwise she would have reamed him out for being an asshole.

Lila still might do that, right after she fucked his brains out.

Tightening the laces on her running shoes, she stepped out into the weight room and quickly found the object of her lust. Stretched out on the weight bench, Kyle was cranking out a series of bench presses with ease. From this angle Lila could see the sheen of sweat covering his biceps, his calves and thighs, the tremble in his body as he pushed himself past the limits of what most people would consider attempting. Typical Kyle. Never letting anyone, not even his body, tell him what he could do.

The clang of metal on metal filled the room as he dropped the weight bar back onto the rack and sat up. He lifted his tank top, wiping the sweat from his eyes with the material, exposing his hard abs to her. His face bore the scars of years in the cage. His nose was crooked from having been repeatedly broken. The long scar down his cheek wasn't clearly visible from this distance, but she still knew it was there.

Shit, he was beautiful. Not that she'd ever say that to him. No frigging way.

She caught his attention as he stood. Lila swallowed down her nervousness and gave him a little wave. "Hi there."

"What are you doing here?" No preamble, no pleasantries. "We finished your sessions last week."

"Yeah, I know. Mike out front said it was okay. I know you're probably getting ready to go home for the night."

"I was doing my workout." His black hair was cropped short against his head, a conservative look that didn't quite mesh with his too-direct personality. "Mike closing up?"

His direct stare pierced her, making her squirm and her nipples harden. "I think so. The place is empty." It was the main reason she'd come on a Monday night. She'd learned the ebb and flow of the client base over the past year, and this was the only time she figured would work. Neutral ground, but no distractions.

Bracing his hands on his hips, Kyle lowered his chin and narrowed his gaze. "Are you okay?"

The little confession she'd spent a week preparing evaporated from her memory. "Um, I wanted to talk to you about something."

Kyle crossed the room, swallowing the distance in four wide strides. He was barefoot, but that didn't make him any less intimidating. She'd seen the damage he could do with a round-house kick to someone's face.

Lila knew she should be talking, explaining that no matter how hard she'd tried, she couldn't get Kyle out of her dreams. No, dreams were too pedestrian a description. Those were hard-core erotic fantasies, starring her and a very dominant personal trainer.

Lila showering, surprised when Kyle would come in and fuck her. Lila finishing a workout, only to have Kyle demand she drop to her knees and suck his cock. Being at home, surprised when it was Kyle at her door, demanding to be let in.

She had it bad and she didn't have a clue what to do about it.

Looking up into his brown gaze, Lila knew she only had one chance to do this right. Direct and to the point. It was the only thing he'd appreciate. Taking a deep breath, she straightened up, widened her stance slightly and steeled her nerve.

"I'm attracted to you." There. That wasn't so hard. "And I can't seem to get you out of my mind."

Kyle cocked an eyebrow. "Oh?"

"Yeah. I'm sure that happens a lot to you. Clients developing a bit of a crush and all that. And I know you probably had groupies from the circuit. I kept telling myself that it's normal to have a thing for the man who helped me recover my body. I mean, you deal with attractive people every day, and I know there are professional considerations too. You can't sleep with a client and everything. But we finished our sessions, and I've actually switched gyms too. And even if nothing can happen between us, I wanted to let you know. That I'm attracted to you. So...yeah."

At some point during her ramblings, Lila had dropped her gaze and was now staring at his chest. Sweat had soaked through the thin cotton, and she could see the contour of his pecs. His nipples were hard and his deep breathing pressed them against the fabric. She wanted to touch them, lick the salt off his skin. Beg him to touch her.

"Look at me."

Lila complied without thinking, her gaze snapping back to his. Her lips parted and she fought a moan when she saw the raw hunger coming from him. He hadn't shaved. The thick stubble accentuated his square jaw and cheeks, making the spidery scars on his face stand out.

Kyle stepped forward, and instinctively she retreated an equal distance. "Yes?"

Kyle stepped closer again, causing her to retreat once more. Another two steps and Lila found her back pressed against the wall. The concrete blocks were cold against her bare back, but it did little to stem the rush of hot desire rolling through her. Kyle placed a hand on either side of her head, pinning her in place. The cords of muscles rippled as he flexed. Everything about him was rock hard—his body, demeanor, even the vibe he threw off. It didn't matter; Lila wanted him.

"Say it again." His voice was low, commanding in the same way he'd yell at her to do another five push-ups, urge her on to do three more reps with the weights, push her to run another half mile. "Lila."

"I'm attracted to you." She wanted to swallow past the sudden dryness in her mouth, but she couldn't make her body comply.

"Why did you choose me as your trainer?"

It was an odd question, but she saw that the answer was important to him. "You were recommended by my physiotherapist. He said that he couldn't do anything else for me, and that I needed to build my muscle strength."

The car accident had taken a lot out of her, both mentally and physically. She'd given up on herself for a very long time, gained weight, lived with the pain until Kyle came along and gave her the push she needed to reclaim her life.

"I'd wanted to give up on myself so much over the past year, but you kept me going." She dropped his gaze once more, unable to handle the intensity any longer. "I didn't want to disappoint you."

Kyle took her chin in his hand and lifted it. "Not possible."

Shit, there was no way she'd be able to be with someone like Kyle. He was the most attractive man she'd ever met. She'd seen the way the women at the gym would preen whenever he walked into the room, the way conversation brightened when he drew close. Hell, even the other men would work a little harder when he came close. Not that Kyle responded to any of it. Which was...odd. "Am I making a fool of myself? Of course I am. I should go."

"You came here tonight to tell me you were attracted to me." Kyle leaned in until his mouth hovered above her ear. "Did you think I was going to fuck you?"

Lila's chest tightened as she sucked in a breath. The scent of sweat and Kyle's soap filled her senses. It was familiar, equal parts comforting and arousing. Her pussy tingled and grew wet when he nipped at the top of her ear.

"Fuck?" She couldn't manage more than a whisper. "I..."

"Did you want to see if you could get me out of your system? Scratch the itch?" He lowered his mouth so his lips brushed the side of her neck. "You want to touch my body the way you've wanted to for months? See if my muscles are as hard as they look?"

"Christ," she muttered. "I don't know."

"I do." He came closer, pressing his thighs to hers. There was no mistaking the erection hard against her belly. "I don't fuck clients. Never. I don't normally fuck former clients either."

Lila squeezed her fingers against the wall. She wanted to touch him, run her fingers through his black hair, scratch her nails down his back as he ground her pussy against his cock. If she moved, there would be nothing holding back the wave of desire she'd dammed up for months now.

Kyle moved one hand from the wall to the side of her neck. He didn't touch her skin, letting it hover an inch above. "You're not a typical client. I want you."

Her head spun as the meaning of his words sunk in. "You... do?"

"I'm not used to holding back with women. I watched you fight to reclaim your life, your body. You transformed before my eyes. You weren't doing it for me, but for yourself. Every time you kept going and fought through the pain, I respected you a bit more. Not everyone has that inner strength." He finally lowered his mouth to her neck and licked the skin. "It turns me on."

Her eyes slipped shut, and she knew she was about to lose all semblance of control. But she had one last question before she'd finally allow herself to give into the temptation. "Why didn't you say anything?"

His chuckle tickled her throat. "You were paying me. I'm not a whore. But now that we're done and I know you're interested..."

The pressure of his teeth on her neck pulled a moan from her. Lila forced her hands from the wall and finally did what she'd dreamed of for months. His strands of hair were soft against her fingers as she pulled him hard against her. It was the only push he needed. Growling, he wrapped his arms around her and sucked her skin.

Yes.

Kyle pulled her from the wall, lifting her up so Lila could wrap her legs around his waist. Sweat from his tank top dampened her chest as he held her fast against him. "I'm going to fuck you here. In this room."

This was better than any fantasy she'd ever had. His hands cupped her ass as he carried her over to the weight bench. Lila sucked in a breath as he deposited her on the still-damp padding. He looked like a dangerous giant, looming over her. Without a word he stripped his tank top from his body, tossing it to the floor. His body bore the marks of a life in the ring. Marred skin from wounds he'd sustained, bruises from training that never seemed to fade. A painting of beauty and pain on living flesh.

"There are things I've wanted to do to you." His gaze slipped from her mouth to her chest. "Things I'm going to do tonight."

Lila squeezed her legs together, increasing the pressure against her clit. She was an educated, successful woman. She shouldn't want this, the need to let this powerful man possess her, consume her body and mind. But she did. For once in her life she didn't question the reasons and just went with it. "Please."

Her voice was soft, trembling with anticipation. "Yes."

"Take that off." Pointing at her bra, Kyle never took his gaze from hers. "Now."

Lila didn't hesitate. Mike might still be there, the cleaners could show up, but she really didn't give a shit. Kyle wanted her, and she wasn't about to say no. She had no shame regarding her body. He'd seen her in far worse shape than she was currently, and not once had he made her feel embarrassed. She was used to having his appraising gaze on her.

"Stand up. Yoga pants off too."

She'd forgone wearing any underwear. Her fingers wrapped around the waistband, and she pulled the tight fabric down slowly. Making sure to bend at the waist, Lila stuck her ass out as she pulled her sneakers and pants off. Standing once more, she found she couldn't meet his gaze.

Kyle grabbed her chin once again. "You're stronger than that. Look me in the eyes."

The urge to answer with a *Sir, yes sir* was overwhelming. Instead, she nodded. "Okay."

Instead of kissing her, touching her, pretty much doing any of the things she wanted, Lila watched as Kyle walked over to his gym bag and pulled out a towel. He laid it out on one of the exercise mats before turning to face her.

"Get over here and give me twenty push-ups."

What the hell? "Pardon?"

Kyle crossed his arms. "You're not going to wuss out on me, are you?"

Oh, screw him. Naked, Lila scooted across the room and dropped to her knees on the towel. "How many?"

"Twenty. And not girl push-ups either."

Stretching her body into the position, Lila braced her hands under her shoulders, got her toes under her and pushed her body up. It was a single, smooth motion, her body a ridged plank as she moved. It should have felt weird doing naked push-ups for her trainer, but Lila quickly realized he was using this as some sort of fantasy fulfillment of his own. Who was she to burst his bubble?

It wasn't until the third up move that he touched her. Large hands cupped her ass, squeezed as she lowered her body back to the floor. Fingers dug into her cheeks, spreading her ass open. Lila's face flamed and her arms shook.

"That's only three." He slapped her ass.

Lila managed to push her body back up as he continued to fondle her. His fingers shifted lower, squeezing her hamstrings, sneaking in between her legs to caress the sensitive flesh. There was no way she'd be able to keep going, not with his hands all over her, teasing her body as he stoked her lust.

"Stop." He put a hand on her back when she finished her tenth push-up. "Spread your legs apart and put your hands greater than shoulder length apart. Next five this way."

Lila knew her face was red, between the strain, desire and embarrassment; there was no way it couldn't be. He would see her pussy now, wet from her arousal. She needed him to put his hands on the places where she needed him most—her cunt, breasts, pinching her nipples until she screamed with pleasure.

Kyle moved to stand by her head. With a single push, his shorts fell to pool at his feet. He kicked them away, along with his sneakers and socks. Now they were both naked. It should have been an even playing ground, but as Lila cranked out push-up number fifteen, she knew nothing was further from the truth.

"Push and hold at the top of the move."

She did so, but her arms began to shake almost instantly.

He got to his knees beside her, and simultaneously reached

for her breast and between her legs. "I'll tease you for as long as you can maintain this position."

Not fair!

The slide of his finger between her pussy lips had Lila crying out. Everything felt amplified, every brush of skin against skin.

Kyle pinched her nipple as he thrust two fingers into her cunt. "Every time you'd bend over, lie back on a bench, spread your legs as you stretched, I wanted to do this. Touch you, make you moan. Fuck you until you begged me for more." He began to thrust his fingers into her, matching the rhythm with the tweaks on her nipple. "I'm going to fuck you, but not until you're begging for me."

"Please, Kyle." Her arms couldn't take much more of this. "I need you."

"Show me how much." He turned his hand so his fingers pressed against her G-spot. "Suck my cock."

"Yes." Tears filled her eyes and her nose threatened to run. "Anything."

He pulled his fingers from her pussy, leaving her hungry for more. "You can drop."

The relief in her muscles was instantaneous. Not that he gave her any time to relax and enjoy it. The next thing she knew, Kyle was tugging her by the shoulders, getting her up on her knees as he stood. His cock, larger than that of any man she'd been with before, was red and leaking with precum. She could smell how turned-on he was.

Putting a hand to the back of her head, Kyle encouraged her forward. The thought of leaving never once entered her mind. This was what she wanted, who she wanted and exactly how she wanted it to happen.

Sticking her tongue out, Lila licked a trail from the base of his balls up his shaft to the head of his cock. The salty tang of the precum set her mouth watering. She needed more. Opening as wide as she could, she swallowed down as much as she could handle.

The girth of his shaft forced her to keep her mouth wider than was comfortable. Closing her eyes, she focused on giving Kyle what he wanted, licking and sucking as much as she could. She would pause to tease the prominent vein on the underside of his cock, before switching to suck hard on the head. When she didn't think she could continue on, Lila used her hands to pump him hard.

"That's it. You keep going even when you don't think you can. You've got a soul of iron under that beautiful heart of yours. Suck me down."

Lila groaned, her mind slipped away, leaving behind all the details of her life that plagued her. Her health, her job, the insecurities of not knowing where to go from here. None of that mattered while she was with Kyle.

"Enough." He tugged her head back. Lifting her chin once more, he ran a thumb across her lips. "You're so fucking beautiful. Lie back."

Stretching out on her back felt amazing, easing the ache from her muscles. Kyle lifted her legs and threw them over his shoulders. With no preamble, he lowered his mouth to her pussy and sucked her clit. Lila groaned and buried a hand in his hair.

His tongue circled her, licking the seam between her lips as he slipped his fingers into her cunt. Lila couldn't get her brain to register that this was actually happening. That Kyle was doing this to *her*. Her brain short-circuited and the rest of her thoughts evaporated as he set up a punishing pace.

He fucked her with his fingers, pressing against her G-spot with an inward curl. She'd never had a man drive her this close to orgasm so quickly. Standing on the precipice of her release,

Lila squeezed her fingers in his hair, the only warning she could muster.

Kyle growled and sucked harder on her clit. It was too much for her to handle, and Lila stopped trying to fight it.

"God!"

Her grip on his hair locked hard, as waves of pleasure hijacked her body. She couldn't move or breathe as her orgasm flared through her, consuming every inch. Kyle pulled his face back, but continued to pump his fingers into her pussy. Another wave of her orgasm hit, and with it came a jet of cum from her body. Lila screamed, unable to fight the powerful pleasure, shocked at what he'd been able to do to her.

"I knew you had that in you. A squirter."

Lila looked up at him and blinked. "What...I...god..." Okay, so talking wasn't a good idea.

He didn't seem to mind. Kyle grinned down, running a hand along the inside of her thigh. "Not all women can do that. It's fucking hot."

She couldn't stop from chuckling. "Glad I could go the extra mile for you."

"I never doubted you could."

He reached for the condom that he'd brought over with the towel. Holding it up, he cocked an eyebrow at her. "Ready for more?"

"Yes." She'd never get enough of him. Especially now.

With sure fingers, he tore open the package and quickly rolled the condom down his shaft. Kyle lined himself up and thrust in, filling her completely. Before Lila had a chance to adjust, he grabbed her around the waist and pulled her up as he sat back on his heels.

"Ride me. Hard."

Lila shifted so her feet were flat on the floor, giving her the leverage she needed. Wrapping her arms around his neck, she began to fuck herself on his cock. The angle had him driving deeply into her and they quickly fell into a rhythm, fucking and grinding against each other. Kyle's arms were wrapped around her, his hand bracing the back of her neck as he devoured her mouth.

It was strange being on top of him this way, their bodies pressed flush as he fucked up into her. He was a powerful man, strong in body and will. She was little more than a humming-bird compared to him, and yet here she was reducing him to a series of grunts and moans.

"Need you to come again." He spoke the words against her lips. "Want to feel you squeeze my cock."

Lila lowered her face to his shoulder and slammed her body down hard against his. Her clit rubbed against his pubic hair on every stroke, teasing the already sensitized flesh. His words were a command that her body desperately wished to comply with.

Kyle tipped her back slightly, giving him access to her breasts. When his mouth found her nipple, Lila felt a corresponding pulse of pleasure echo in her pussy. Shit, she really was going to come again.

Closing her eyes, Lila concentrated on the feel of Kyle's mouth on her breast, the way his cock stretched and filled her. She started to moan, to gasp, desperately in need of more air as her head spun.

"That's it, baby."

With a moan, she dropped her forehead to his shoulder and slammed down onto him as she came a second time. It was too much, too strong, and her body fell limp against him.

Kyle squeezed her tightly to his chest as he drove up into her body. He bit down on her shoulder, licking and nipping as he moaned. "Gonna come. Fuck yeah."

He squeezed her hard as he slammed into her a few times more before he cried out. His muscles shook beneath her, but he didn't waver until his orgasm finished. Finally, they slipped back to the towel, wrapped in each other's arms, covered in sweat and panting hard.

"Wow," Lila finally managed to whisper. "That was... amazing."

Kyle chuckled. "I think I'm done with my workout for the night."

"Sorry about that."

"Never apologize for great sex. Ever."

They lay there for a few minutes until the air conditioner sent a blast of cool air across them.

"I better get you up." He ran a hand along her back. "You'll freeze in here."

Lila had never had sex like this before, not only in such a public location, but with a man like Kyle. She didn't want it to end, to slip away from reality into the haze of memory, the only thing to keep her warm during the lonely nights.

"Did you want to have a shower?" He kissed the top of her head.

"Yeah, that would be good." Damn, this was it. Soon she'd be leaving and Kyle would be gone from her life for good.

"Hey." He bumped her forehead with his nose, forcing her to look up. "What's wrong?"

"I..." She shrugged.

"You think I'm kicking you out?" There was nothing goofy about the grin he gave her. "You think after a year of being your trainer, of having to force myself to hold back for fear of doing something ethically wrong with one of my clients that I'd never forgive myself for; that after you telling me you're attracted to me and the awesome sex we just had, I'm going to let you go?" He chuckled.

Okay, that wasn't quite what she was expecting. Not that Lila was about to complain. "You're not?"

"I think you know me well enough by now to realize that when there's something I want, I don't sit by and let it get away from me."

"No," she returned his grin, "you don't."

"I'm not about to let you become the exception to that rule. Until otherwise notified, you're mine."

Lila shivered, loving the possessive tone. Yeah, she had it bad.

"Now, I'm going to have a shower with you, and then we are going to go back to my place. I think a conversation is in order." He lowered his mouth to hers and kissed her softly on the lips. "And then more fucking."

Her heart raced and Lila knew that her determination hadn't failed her. She'd fought through her self-doubt and had been rewarded with the ultimate prize—a man who not only wanted her but respected her.

It was everything Lila could have hoped for.

With a quick kiss of her own, she cupped his cheek. "Yes, sir."

DIVING DEEP

Jenny Lyn

Sitting on the bottom of a pool was akin to being back inside the womb, I suspected. In the dark, cocooned by thousands of gallons of warm water, I heard nothing but the slow sounds of my breaths hissing through the diving regulator in my mouth. No boisterous family conversations backed by tacky holiday music to make your ears bleed. No twenty-five sticky, rambunctious kindergarteners demanding my full attention all at the same time. Just blessed silence and me. Even my thoughts had quieted.

Why hadn't I thought of this hiding place sooner?

If my brother knew I'd swiped some of his scuba gear, he'd be pissed. But it was a risk I was willing to take to escape the throng of over-sauced relatives inside my parents' house where every other question was about my relationship status. Or rather, my lack of one. When I'd spotted Devin's diving equipment in the utility room while shoving a bag of garbage into the trash can, it was too much of a godsend to resist.

The family pool was blissfully heated and far enough away from the main house for me not to be discovered stripping to my underwear and slipping into the deep end. The mask didn't fit perfectly, but at least it kept the chlorine from stinging my eyes and water from going up my nose. I knew just enough about operating the scuba gear to prevent myself from drowning and remain where I was for at least another fifteen precious minutes, thanks to the help of the weight I'd strapped around my ankle.

Or so I'd thought.

I spotted him looming above me on the edge of the pool deck, his body silhouetted by the landscape lighting surrounding the trees and shrubbery. The rippling water distorted his shape, but I'd still recognize Jake blindfolded. The wide shoulders tapering to a narrow waist, the imposing height and size of him.

He hadn't yet arrived for the party when I'd slipped away. I should probably have been flattered he'd sought me out over the company of my brother, his best friend. I would have been if I hadn't known that his visit was only going to lead to more misery for me in the end.

I remained very still while he put the puzzle pieces together, hands braced on his hips as he looked around, even going so far as to hold my breath so no bubbles broke the surface.

The water nearest the bottom would be dark since I hadn't bothered turning on the pool lights. Soon enough, though, he would spot my discarded clothing and shoes. The air in my lungs began to burn before it broke from my mouth around the regulator, sending a shimmering cluster of bubbles floating upward like millions of tiny diamonds.

Jake's SEAL training immediately took over. I watched as he jerked his shoes off, stripped out of his jacket and shirt, and dove into the water. The realization I wasn't actually drowning took about three seconds. Even the near darkness at the bottom of the pool couldn't obscure the expression on his face, anger rapidly chasing away worry. Then I was being dragged to the surface whether I wanted to go or not.

He tossed the scuba gear onto the deck as if it weighed no more than a marshmallow. The heavy chunk of lead strapped around my ankle kept trying to pull me back under until he unbuckled it and tossed it aside too. I stripped off the mask, adding it to the pile.

I was now trapped between Jake's big body and the side of the pool. Long, muscled arms caged me in while our ragged breaths heated each other's faces. I tried not to stare at his chest, tried harder not to think about how badly I wanted to sip the water from his smooth golden skin.

"What the fuck, Katie?" He passed a hand over his wet face in agitation. "Were you trying to give me a heart attack?"

"You practically have gills."

Jake glared. Tiny droplets clung to his obscenely long eyelashes and sparkled in the light. He was so handsome it gave *me* heart palpitations when I looked at him.

"That's not even remotely funny. You know what I meant."

"I'm sorry," I lied.

"No, you're not. But you're about to be."

Before I could ask what that could possibly mean, I was being lifted out of the water, slung over his shoulder like a sack of potatoes and hauled out of the pool.

I squirmed uselessly against the iron band around my thighs. "Jake, put me down!"

"I will in a minute." He kept walking.

If my upside-down bearings were correct, he was headed for the pool house.

I didn't want to be alone in there with him. A certain memory had been created in that miniature apartment years ago, and it would weaken my resolve the second we passed through the door, especially when both of us were half-naked and dripping wet.

"Okay, I'm genuinely sorry I scared you," I said. "Now please let me go so I can put some clothes on. It's cold as ice in here." That *wasn't* a lie. Gooseflesh rose on my arms, and my nipples pinched tight inside my flimsy bra.

He turned the deadbolt behind us before sinking down onto the couch with me sprawled across his thick thighs. "I'm about to warm you up."

"What?" I squeaked before his hand came down hard on my ass. "Ow! Dammit, that hurt! What are you doing?"

He spanked me twice more, landing a slap on each cheek.

The pain made tears sting my eyes.

"Maybe being around five-year-olds all day is starting to rub off on you." *Whap.*

That blow caused me to wince and dig my fingernails into the couch cushion and my teeth into my bottom lip.

My ass was on fire. He'd done what he promised, though; I wasn't exactly cold anymore. More disturbing was the deep throb working its way down through my hips, settling some-place it shouldn't, turning into something dangerous.

Wait a minute. Had he just...? "Did you just call me a child?"

"I implied you were acting like one." One more vicious slap and his hand stayed pressed to the bottom curve of my over-heated bottom, resting there, waiting for me to sass him some more no doubt. But then it started to slide up, up, up, toward the top of my panties. "No one could ever look at you, honey, and think child."

Oh, I wished he wouldn't say things like that. It fucked with my head. Being stretched across his lap, completely at his mercy, fucked with my body. There was nothing left to fight back with.

That venturing hand made its way inside my underwear. "Jake?"

Ever so slowly, my panties were pushed out of his way until they rested at the tops of my thighs in a damp twisted mess. One wide palm caressed me, soothing the sting. My face flamed as hot as the skin on my ass.

"We shouldn't be in here...doing...whatever it is you're thinking about doing," I offered in weak protest.

If he touched me where I thought he was about to touch me, it would all be over. Every shred of progress I'd made in trying to get over him once and for all while he was away would be gone in the stroke of a finger. It wasn't fair he had this kind of hold on me, and I wasn't ashamed to admit, to myself at least, that I resented it.

"What's wrong with where we're at, Katie? The greatest moment of my life happened right here on this very couch six years ago, almost to the day."

Hearing him say that did me in. My resistance left in such a rush I almost felt lightheaded in the aftermath. All this time I'd thought losing our virginity together had meant more to me than it did to him. The reverence in his voice said differently. And what was the point in trying to fight it anyway? We were both single adults, certainly hot for each other. Sweet Christ, the lust between us was nearly tangible. We proved that every time he came home on leave.

It was the scarcity that was killing me. I couldn't keep wanting more and resenting not being able to have it. I couldn't keep holding out for someone who didn't want permanence, or at the very least commitment, as much as I did. Yet I had no right to demand it. What was I left with except heartache?

He unhooked my bra and rolled me over on his lap. My underwear was stripped away, leaving me naked and vulnerable. I burrowed farther into the plump cushions while he slid out from under my legs and struggled to remove his wet jeans.

It was such a gift to look at him naked. Jake's body was a work of art, sculpted and strong. It deserved to be immortalized in bronze and displayed in a museum somewhere. People should have to pay money to stare at it and be thankful for the experience. I would, even though I was lucky enough to be able to close my eyes and recall it whenever I wanted.

Just when my gaze settled on his equally beautiful cock, he flipped me onto my stomach and straddled my calves. His hands smoothed up the backs of my thighs, stopping at the bottom curve of my ass. "Still hurt?" he asked, humor lacing his voice.

"Will you kiss it and make it better if I say yes?"

Instead, he bit me.

I yelped and tried to roll away, but his hands held my hips firmly in place. Then his tongue was tracing a path up my spine while he worked his fingers into me from behind. I could hold very still then and let him work his magic on my clit. I could hold my breath while he fucked me with two thick digits and made me roll my pelvis to help things along. I could, and I did so he wouldn't stop. When he had me panting and embarrassingly wet, teetering on the brink of coming, he pulled away again. I clenched my teeth together to trap a needy plea for more.

I heard him rummaging in his wet jeans, cursing a soaked wallet, then the crinkle of the condom wrapper. He jerked my hips up and made me spread my knees so he could fit between them. When I started to push up on my hands, one of his shoved me back down.

Damp clumps of my hair fell across my face, hiding my grin. Yeah, I liked Jake like this. Pushy and demanding. Rough.

Almost greedy. Tonight, I deserved it for scaring him the way I did. And whatever form of erotic punishment he decided to dole out, I wanted all of it.

There was no easing inside my pussy. No, he thrust hard and deep. So deep it hurt a little and forced a groan that started somewhere near the soles of my feet. He pulled out slowly and pushed back in, over and over again, until I felt everything inside me tighten.

Jake knew that too. His fingers pressed into my hips hard enough to leave bruises, and I came in a blinding, shuddering rush. A few more harsh thrusts and he stilled as he emptied inside of me.

Jake's tight grip on my hips loosened. He leaned down, dropping kisses across my shoulder before he pulled away.

I rolled to my side and watched to see if he got dressed to leave.

But he grabbed a blanket from the back of an armchair and draped it over me, then gathered up his jeans and my underwear and tossed them in the dryer.

"Scoot over," he said from the side of the couch.

I shifted to the edge so he could spoon me.

Jake brushed my hair aside and kissed my neck. "Why were you hiding at the bottom of the pool, Katie?"

"Have you been inside the house yet? It's like a three-ring circus in there. I'll take a classroom full of screaming five-year-olds over the family any day of the week."

"But why the pool? Why not hide out in here?"

I sighed into the blanket. "You know why."

His arm tightened around my waist, but he didn't comment.

"Devin will be mad that you're not spending any time with him."

Jake rose up on one elbow, frowning down at me. "Are you trying to get rid of me?"

Maybe. "No. It's not that. It's just…" I shrugged and picked at invisible lint on the couch cushion.

"Goddammit, Katie, look at me." When I did, he pushed harder. "It's just what?"

Something inside me broke wide open and words came rushing through the crevice left behind. "I can't keep doing this, Jake. I can't." I shook my head and scrambled into the corner of the couch, pulling my knees up to my chest. "I see you every couple of months, we spend hours upon hours in bed—the sex is amazing, don't get me wrong—but then you leave and take my heart with you when you go, and it's killing me! I know you've never asked me for anything exclusive, and I've never pushed you for more either, but I'm ready for that now. Since you're not, we need to end this."

"No."

I fought back tears. "Please, Jake, don't make this any harder than it already is."

He scrambled off the couch, holding one finger up. "Wait right there, okay? Don't move a muscle. I'll be right back."

He darted into the pool house's tiny bathroom and came out with a beach towel wrapped around his waist, then headed to the washroom door.

"Where are you going?"

He left me sitting there in the quiet, wondering. The only thing keeping the room from being completely dark was a small sliver of moonlight streaming in through a gap in the curtains. I watched his shadow pass it before returning with our discarded clothing.

After digging inside his jacket pockets, he came back to me, crouching down beside the couch, and opened his fist. A small black velvet box sat in his palm.

I swallowed hard. "Jake?"

"I might take your heart with me when I leave, Katie, but you've had mine since the first moment I laid eyes on you. And every single time I leave, it's *my* heart that stays behind with you."

The tiny box and his face grew blurry before the tears spilled down my cheeks.

"Open the box, honey."

Leaving it perched in his hand, I slowly lifted the lid. Inside was the most beautiful emerald-cut diamond ring ever made. Just a single stone on a platinum band nestled against a background of onyx. I tore my eyes away from it to look up at him. "Is that what I think it is?"

"I never meant for you to think I was stringing you along all this time. Honestly, I can't believe my luck that you've waited until now to try and give me the boot. So, in answer to your question, I guess it depends. If you think it's something I'm going to slide on your finger like a placeholder or an appeasement, you'd be wrong. But if you think it's my way of saying I love you and I want to spend the rest of my life proving it to you, then you'd be right."

I flung myself on top of him. We landed in a tangled heap on the floor, blankets and towels twisted around our bodies, my cheeks wet with tears and his mouth on mine.

When we finally came up for air, he said, "I pictured this happening a lot differently, you know. I was going to take you out to a nice, romantic dinner with candles and flowers then pop the question when we got back to my place. We'd probably still be naked, though."

I giggled against his neck while he slid the ring onto my left hand. I held it up, letting it catch fire in the moonlight. "We generally are naked when we're together."

"You had to go and ruin my plan by pretending to be Jacques Cousteau. I think you shaved ten years off my life, so thanks for that too. Might have to take early retirement now."

The smile faded from my face when he brought up the subject of his work. Well, Jake didn't see it as work, really. He loved the Navy, loved being a SEAL even more.

"How long are you home for this time?"

He rolled me beneath him, burying his face in the curve of my shoulder. "A while."

I scowled at the ceiling. "Cute. How long is 'a while'?"

That mouth of his was magic. The more it moved toward my breast, the less I was capable of coherent thought. "Could be forever," he mumbled against my skin.

Grasping his face in my hands, I forced him to look at me. "Explain please."

"I put in for an instructor position. I'm about ninety-nine-percent positive I'll get it."

"Seriously?" My heart beat wildly inside my chest. As selfish as it was of me to hope for, I wanted him out of combat so badly my body ached. I also knew that he didn't do anything he wasn't certain about. He wasn't doing this to placate me; he was doing it because he was ready for a change. Finally, he was ready for *us*.

"Of course I'm serious. Besides, if I leave you again, you're liable to drown yourself."

I smacked him on the arm then kissed him, long and wet and deep. "I love you too, you know."

He gave me a slow, confident smile. "You wouldn't have waited this long for me if you didn't."

HEATED NEGOTIATIONS

Macy Man

Paige clutched a fistful of Abercrombie-style button-down and pivoted.

The college boy, who smelled of cheap whiskey, completed his decent headfirst to the concrete without taking her along for the ride.

Bobbing around his friends, who all looked as cute and just as wasted, she continued winding though the crowd. While most around her craned their necks toward the sky, mouths agape at the colorful spectacle of friendly little bombs, she kept her target in view. The Fourth of July crush of one million warm, Detroit bodies wasn't enough to deter her lust for vengeance. It had been twenty-four hours since she'd been royally fucked and reaped no pleasure from the experience. Tonight, she would get release.

The security guard working the door of the City-County Building nodded at Paige's badge, and she stomped through the lobby. Up the elevator and down a corridor of cubicle-sized offices, Paige saw the door labeled ROOF ACCESS in the distance. After the echo of two ground-eating strides in its direction, the door swung wide with a metal smack, and two Special Response Team members in full tactical gear strode into the hallway.

At the sight of the blacked-out commandos, their faces obscured by balaclavas and bodies loaded down with Kevlar and weaponry, adrenaline shot through her veins like a bullet from a gun. All thoughts of fatigue from lack of sleep over the past forty-eight hours or the hour and a half it took warring through the crowd to get here vanished.

Shoulders back and chin up, she stopped directly in front of the two men. "Donovan Wolfe?"

Two sets of eyes went wide followed by heads shaking. The tallest of the two hitched a thumb toward the access door.

Paige inclined her head, a small gesture of thanks, and pushed past them.

One of the men, no way to know which since she wasn't looking, cleared his throat. "Sergeant Cline, should we call an ambulance?"

The corners of her mouth turned up when she replied without glancing back, "No. Call the medical examiner." Behind her the metal door slammed shut cutting off the men's *oohs* and chuckles.

Outside the cover of the building, Paige was surprised by the otherworldliness of the rooftop. Wailing sirens and honking horns were muted by the height and whipping wind, which took her hair in a violent gust and slapped it across her face. On any other night, she could lose herself up here, but tonight she couldn't allow any distractions. Inhaling deeply, she focused.

Two more SRT members occupied the tar-topped roof. One big mother stood, legs braced apart, leaning loosely against the building's wide ledge where he studied the ground below through the scope of his SR-90. The other crouched his more meager, yet respectable frame on the sleek black epoxy, stowing his gear.

Coordination between the negotiator and the SRT funneled through the commander. So Paige had never met the elite leader of the Special Response Team she sought. Both men's faces were hidden from view, yet she knew which of the two bore the name Wolfe. She'd heard through the department the former Special Forces officer always went the extra mile for his country. Here he was again, working harder than his men, leading by example.

Wasn't he special.

Paige ignored the hint of respect that bubbled up in her mind and tried to hate him for it. Quickly, her rage came back in the form of a roar in the night. "Donovan Wolfe!"

Her voice rang in her own ears, but the behemoth didn't look up, didn't shift in the slightest. For a split second she wondered if the wind carried off her demand before it could make it to his ears, but then she looked at his buddy whose eyes met hers in a flash before they returned to his gear and he packed the last of it in a flurry of movement.

The man stood, nodded at her and made for the door, calling over his shoulder to Wolfe, "*Dios bendice*, my man."

Still the son of a bitch didn't move.

The metal door slammed once more, closing the two of them out together. Against clenched fists, Paige fought the urge to close the distance at a run and check him into the ledge—or better yet pitch him over the side.

But no, this could be one of the most critical negotiations of her career, and she'd do it right. Hell, she'd talked a furious cabbie into surrendering himself and his two hostages this morning. How hard could this be?

* * *

He'd spotted her in his scope an hour ago. Her cheeks flushed to a lovely pink from effort, and likely fury, as she used sleek arms and agile feet to weave through the festive crowd below. His cock had jumped when he'd watched her pouty mouth purse and thin as she worked her way toward him. As she came for him.

Primed as her body was for a fight, he'd enjoy pushing her to her limits, preparing her body for his. From anger. To frustration. To lust. Unethical to the max, especially given the reason she was here, but fuck if he cared. For too long Donovan had watched through the distance of his scope, tempted by her fierce nature, innate skill, and a body made for his indulgence. Even now, as she waited for him to move, acknowledge her presence, say something, he played her.

As leader of the SRT, he'd read every report of her negotiations since she'd started with the DPD. For the safety of his men he needed to know their negotiator was competent.

Time after time she'd impressed him with her calm authority in extreme stress situations. When others would have thrown in the towel, she hunkered down with bared teeth or kisses, whichever the situation called for, to peacefully resolve the entanglement of madness, weapons and innocent lives. And though no negotiator liked to relinquish control and call for force, she executed the call without hesitation when necessary.

Regardless of all her ability in the field, he'd break her tonight. In the sweetest fashion, he'd make her come under him in every way possible.

The sound of quiet footsteps signaled triumph. After several minutes of stillness, save for the wind, she walked toward him. On a breeze came the smell of her: coffee, Dial soap and sex. He inhaled and held her inside him for as long as he could stand before letting her go. A high, similar to the one he felt after running a marathon, hit hard in his chest and spread throughout his limbs. A groan of satisfaction left his throat.

Paige's reciprocating gasp echoed in his ears and stroked the length of his dick, increasing the pressure against his fatigues.

The group he'd been surveying finally dissipated five minutes later, and he eased to his full height, bringing his weapon off the ledge. Turning his back to her, Donovan walked one step to his bag and began disassembling the SR-90. He figured she'd stay planted where he'd left her, but the sight of gray boots made him smile behind his nylon veil. He laid the Robar down and stroked an ungloved hand down the barrel, his customary show of appreciation for the weapon which had allowed him to save many by taking a few. Her foot twitched like she wanted to kick the gun out of her way and snatch him up by the throat. His smile grew.

In a flash, he was up. Not face-to-face, but chest to the air above her head. He towered over her, leaning into her space. He crowded the air she consumed in a gasp. Her clear blue eyes narrowed to slits as she arched her neck and tried to cover shock with a defiant gaze. Donovan wanted her to retreat one step, so he could advance on her, but her boots stuck to the tar. Challenge upon challenge, she prolonged his amusement.

Her lips parted, the top one curling in a near snarl. "Why would you fuck me like that?"

Even to himself, his voice sounded as though he'd swallowed gravel when he drawled, "How exactly did I fuck you?"

Those plump lips became a mashed line between her teeth, when she, no doubt, realized her error in word choice. Her hair caressed her back and chest as she shook off the implication of his tone or maybe the annoyance he fueled inside her. "You know exactly why I'm here, and I'm not leaving until I get an explanation. You're trying to railroad my career, and I won't allow it."

"Did you come?" he said slowly.

She took a step back. "What?" she asked, her voice pitching high at the end of the word.

"You said I fucked you."

After a silent moment she surged toward him. "I've been through boot camp, hell week, FBI training and a shitty marriage. It's going to take a hell of a lot more than dirty talk to intimidate me. So, cut the crap."

"Did you come?"

"This morning in the shower, but it had nothing to do with you." A confident smirk played over her lips.

He canted his head. "Then I didn't fuck you. If I had, you'd have come again and again, and this morning in the shower you would have been thinking of me on top of you, inside you, filling you, pushing you."

Her smirk fell, and her expression gaped. He watched as her eyes searched his, as her mind tried to calculate the situation and decide upon the best way to handle him.

Using the moment he'd built, Donovan stepped over his bag.

Given the option of being pushed over by his chest or retreat, she chose to step back. Two steps of his and four on her part had her ass against the ledge. Startled, her eyes flew left and right, taking in the glittery skyline. Her head tilted down as she assessed the fall, and then her eyes scanned the rooftop looking for a way out.

He snagged her attention. "Paige, do you want to know why I want you under me?"

Again her eyes searched, but this examination was internal. While she waited for her response, his gaze scoured her head to toe. Her wet lips, heaving breasts, braced legs all begged for him.

After a time her glance locked with his. "Yes," she said just above a whisper.

He took a step closer, his hips crowding her against the ledge. "Contrary to what you believe, I want you under me, with the SRT, because it will save lives. With the commander as a go-between for you, the negotiator, and me, the force team leader, there's too much lag time in critical situations. It provides too much air and opportunity for things to go wrong. Miscommunication. Errors. Deaths of hostages, my men, you.

"You like to go face-to-face with these crazy fucks, which works most of the time. But what happens when it doesn't? I'm not hooked in your ear. The commander is. I need to be in the room, in your ear, in your head.

"Come under me. We'll work together. You'll like it." He emphasized his last point by grinding his hips against her.

A deep belly laugh rolled out her mouth and her lips curved high. "Men. You're either threatened by us or in awe of us. The threatened ones want to control and the awed ones want to watch. You're no different, soldier. You hate that I call the shots at a scene and see an opportunity to change that. Well, I have oodles more training in psych and for negotiations than you, and you won't issue orders to me."

Yes, he would, and she'd follow them.

Donovan planted a palm on either side of the ledge, pinning her in place. Her hands didn't come up to shove him away, which he took as consent. Slowly, he leaned in, passing her lips by a whisper as he moved to her ear. Just below her lobe he bit lightly into her neck and felt the dull thud of her escalating heartbeats. The balaclava's fabric created a protective barrier, and then friction, as he slowly scraped his teeth down her neck, over her collarbone, across her breast to her nipple.

When he bit down through the layers of fabric, she moaned and arched her slender torso against his mouth. Finding it already engorged, he slipped her nipple farther between his teeth, bit down and pulled, sliding the tender flesh through his bite from base to tip, time and again.

When she panted frantically, he stood. "Unbutton your shirt," he ordered in a bark.

Her eyes searched his for the briefest of seconds. "I don't know what you think this is going to prove."

"Maybe nothing. But that doesn't mean you don't want it." He jerked his chin toward her chest. "Unbutton it."

Two petite, shaky hands moved to the top button of her shirt. One by one she unfastened the buttons, steadier hands moving faster at the end. Her lips pursed in a stubborn pout. "What now?"

"Less lip. Take it off."

"You're a sonovabitch, Wolfe." But her shirt parted over a sheer blue bra, cupping small round breasts with aroused centers.

"And the bra," he said more hoarsely this time than he would have liked.

Instantly, her hands went to the clasp at her back. Two breasts extended toward him from the effort, and he greeted them with his covered mouth.

Before long she moaned deep and the begging request slipped from her lips. "Please."

"Please what?" he asked, pausing above her chafed breasts.

"More," she breathed, the word a desperate plea.

He left her breasts and traveled up to her ear. "Tell me exactly what you want me to do to you."

She moaned and ground her pussy against his leg. She tried

to hide her face in his neck when she whispered, "I want—"

He pulled back and pinned her with a steely gaze. "Go on."

She swallowed hard, but met his hard gaze with one of her own, still defiant despite the fact he'd pushed her to bare herself. "I want you to fuck me. I want to be under you—here at least. Now."

Now, *he* begged. "More."

Her eyes closed for a moment, then flashed open, a hint of vulnerability in their moist depths. "I want your mouth on me. You, inside me. I want you to pound me with everything you've got and make me scream so loud when I come that all of Detroit hears my excitement."

His breath came in short strained gusts. He'd asked for this. Dreamed of this, and she was giving him exactly what he wanted. With a quick move, he filled his hands with her buttcheeks, locked their cores together and laid her back on the ledge. Her legs wrapped tight around his torso and dug into his muscled back and cheeks. Before him, she lay bare-breasted, a marvelous painting set against the blackness of the sky and shimmer of city lights.

She rode him through the layers of his clothing as he slid his hands up her body. The first skin-to skin-contact, his hand to her belly, sent a thrill up his arms. Her smooth skin stretched under his calloused hand. He circled her chest, strumming over her erect tips again and again as her breathing became labored, and her legs clamped him harder in time with her undulating thrusts against his clothed erection.

A moaning cry pierced the night sky. "Oh yes!"

She rode it out, mewing and bucking against his throbbing penis. While she calmed, he traced her lips, the object of many fantasies, with his thumb. When her breathing quieted, she lapped her tongue at his finger. She caught it on the third lap between her teeth and sucked hard, pulling him in to the base and working it with her mouth.

When she released it, he demanded, voice rough as ground rock, "More."

She nodded and dropped her legs from his waist. He stepped back while she edged off the ledge to drop to her knees. Donovan's head lolled back at the jerk of his zipper, and he grinned like the fucking Cheshire cat. Perfection. She knew to leave his buckle fastened so his sidearm, knife and ammo stayed put.

Paige's hands were warm as she released him from his pants, and her mouth was hotter still. Slick wet suction welcomed his cock from tip to damn near base as she immediately relaxed her throat and allowed him in deep. With the same enthusiasm with which she'd ridden home her orgasm, she pumped the length and girth of him. The sounds of slurping and moist suction filled his ears. Her hands cupped the sensitive skin of his testicles, massaged and pulled, while her head bobbed.

Tension soon tingled heavy in his balls, rushed up his shaft and released his own climax. Moaning while he groaned, she coveted all he tried to deny her with greedy pulls and gulps.

She stood, gaze raised, but not submitting, and smiled like a devil triumphing over a tempted sinner. Slowly, she licked her smiling lips.

Incited by her smirk, he wound a hand in her blonde locks, and with his body shoved her back against the building's edge. His mouth teased hers, and she licked at him through the balaclava. She bit down on his lip and pulled until she had only material between clamped pearlies, and then yanked aside the material, revealing his mouth.

His eyes clamped shut in ecstasy when their tongues mated. Sweeter than ice cream; with a bite of his own on her lips, he was lost. Spiraled out of control. Driven to the edge. His hands moved to her pants and yanked them down with a frantic movement. Her boots sailed off with a flick of his wrist, and then her gauzy panties and jeans followed. Spreading her ankles wide, he dove down for her core, dying to taste her, to lap up her wetness and invade her with some part of him. Any and every part of him.

Donovan hitched her thighs over his wide shoulders and speared her silken channel with his tongue. Her wetness coated him and filled his mouth with the taste of her. The need for more drove him to withdraw and stroke inward again. His hair was pulled as her hands grasped the covering on his head, but he refused the distraction. Instead, he used his lips to pull on her rosy, swollen clit.

In response, she worked her hips against his face, using her heels against his back for leverage.

Rising, he gripped her asscheeks, arranged her wide open and rubbed his dick from puckered bottom to pointed top, over and over, leaving no part of her intimate skin untouched.

The length of his cock became solid as a rock when she yelled across the city again, calling out to him. "Fuck me. Fuck me. Fuck me."

He repositioned her legs around his hips. Their sexes met. Slick on slick, and there was no waiting. Donovan's hips pushed forward. He slid into her, head to base in a single thrust that left him gasping for air. She fit him like a second skin. A hotter, wetter skin. He pulled out to the tip and rammed home again allowing his balls to smack the damp skin of her ass. Twice more he repeated the ritual, watching as their bodies separated and came together. On the third thrust, he stayed planted deep, enjoying the full contact. He leaned over the ledge, twined his hands in her hair and kissed her hard. Their lips collided, and their tongues curled together in a seductive battle. When he rose, she used her arms to crawl up his body. She latched on with small yet solid arms and legs and began to ride him wildly. Her breasts brushed against his vest. Her sex pumped up and down the length of his straining erection. Widening his stance, he joined in the rhythmic beating of their flesh, his arms throwing her hips into the air, and his cock enjoying gravity's response.

Her clit must have enjoyed the rough ride too, because soon she let loose a series of screams at the sky and a rush of moisture coated his dick. As she spasmed around him, contracting hard, he joined her in orgasm, shouting his triumph at the night.

Though slower, he pumped her still, refusing to leave the pleasure their bodies created. He laid her back on the ledge and rocked inside her while his hands molded her breasts. Every part of her was swollen, moist and red from their efforts. The corners of his mouth went wide in appreciation.

"You know," she said lazily, "you have a killer smile."

"Is that all?"

She shrugged. "Since that's all I've seen, I'll plead the Fifth."

"Fuck many men whose face you've never seen?"

Her eyes widened, like she'd forgotten that little fact.

He almost relented and pulled the covering from his face to reassure her he wasn't an ugly ogre, but her quickly narrowing gaze amused him too much.

Before she had a chance to respond, he flicked her nipples and rolled them between his thumb and forefinger, and then her hips jerked of their own accord. Donovan had just settled into a rooted grind, when two high-pitched beeps breeched their world.

In unison they barked, "Fuck!"

Moving forward, he gave her lips a biting kiss and disengaged their bodies. Quickly, they both retrieved their phones.

Her resplendently naked. Him fully covered, except for his mouth, dick and balls. While accessing the urgent message, he reached into his bag and pulled out a small towel and tossed it to her. With sure reflexes, she caught it and began cleaning while checking her own message.

"Hostage situation four miles from here. You want a ride?"

She laughed hard, doubling over a little. "Didn't I just get one from you?"

"You only want one?" he asked, tone wry.

She gave him that devil's triumphant expression. "No. I want more."

"Good."

"But," she added, "I'm not taking orders from you on scene."

He planted his hands on his hips and leered over her. "You will."

"Only when I'm naked or you're trying to get me that way," she said, fastening the pants she'd pulled up her lean legs.

"We'll see."

With a pouty smirk, she said, "Yes, we will."

ONCE UPON A TIME IN MUKDAHAN

Sidney Bristol

She was going to die. If Emery could have chosen where she would kick the bucket, it wouldn't have been in a muddy pit in the middle of nowhere.

Emery shivered and pressed her back against the side of the soggy pit. There was little shelter from the drizzling rain. Bamboo bars crisscrossed overhead, and a piece of plywood had been thrown over one end. The side of her head throbbed from meeting the butt of a rifle. She was exhausted, tired and hungry. She'd stopped praying that her team back in Thailand would come looking for her. The things she'd seen around the campfire before being tossed in her prison were atrocities she wouldn't wish on her worst enemy.

The top of her prison rose, shaking loose a shower of water droplets. She shivered and hugged herself tighter. One of her kidnappers sneered at her and said something she couldn't translate. She didn't need words to understand what he wanted from her.

Two more men appeared, a large bundle clutched between them. As they shoved it over the edge, she realized it wasn't a thing. The bundle was a person.

She yelped and scrambled sideways as the body splattered mud and water everywhere. The men laughed and yelled more incoherent words. The lid slammed back down, plunging them into semidarkness.

Emery peered over her shoulder. Was he dead? Bile rose up in her throat. Was this the man they'd had strapped between two trees? She squeezed her eyes shut, willing the memory to the darkest recesses of her mind.

The body groaned and mud slurped around limbs as he shifted.

Emery groped around for something, anything to use as a weapon, and grabbed a slippery rock the size of her fist. It wasn't much, but her best friend's brother had shown her a thing or two about making do with what she had in a pinch.

The man sat up, holding one arm to his chest while the other cradled his head. He was big, really big. The pit was only six feet across and he took up more than half.

"Don't come near me. I'm warning you," she blurted. She could hear the fear in her voice, high pitched and frantic.

He pushed to his knees. The clouds must have thickened because she couldn't make out his features, not that there was much to see except for mud. His arm snaked out, and he grabbed her wrist.

Emery jerked, trying to break his hold, but he might as well have been forged from iron. She swung with her right and cracked the rock against the side of his head.

"Fuck all," he grit out between his teeth.

That was English.

She understood English.

"Oh my god," she gasped. Was this another American prisoner? Some other poor soul they'd snatched off the streets of Mukdahan?

"*Emery*, fuck all."

"Matt?"

"Who else is stupid enough to come after you?" He shoved her hand away and lifted his one good hand to touch the side of his head.

Matt was there. Everything would be okay. It was an unrealistic notion but she clung to it. Emery scooted to his side, trying to keep her hands out of the mud and rotting vegetation.

"I'm so sorry. I didn't know it was you." She hadn't cried yet, but her nerves were breaking. She sniffled and felt the first, hot tear coast down her cheek. She swiped her hand on the last clean spot of clothing and reached for him. "You've got mud all over your hand. Let me."

He froze, and for a moment she thought he would push her away. Matt was good at that, putting distance between himself and the people who loved him. Like her. Not that he knew. She'd had a grand plan to tell him on this trip. Or try to.

Instead, he held completely still. This close she could see the faint shine of light in his eyes. He'd always had great eyes, the color of the bluest water, clearest sky, so blue they hurt. With his silent permission, she gently probed the lump with her fingers.

"Skin's not broken. I'm sorry."

"Not too bad." He blinked and glanced away from her.

"What are you doing here? Where's everyone else?" She bit her lip to keep a hundred other questions inside. Another tear stole down her cheek. She was not meant for situations like these.

"What do you think I'm doing?" He turned back to her. "Aw hell, don't cry."

She sniffled again. "I'm so sorry."

The rain began in earnest. One moment they were dusted with light droplets, the next the skies dumped gallons on them. Matt urged her back against the wall and crawled next to her under the overhang.

"If they don't kill us, the water will," he grumbled.

She shivered and scooted closer. He was warm and she was cold. Even when the sun had been up for a few hours, she hadn't really thawed out. Matt shifted, no doubt uncomfortable with her sitting on his left side, but she didn't care. She was scared and he was there.

"Come here." He sounded resigned as he looped his arm over her shoulder.

Emery burrowed under his jacket. How often had she dreamt of doing exactly this? She didn't know him anymore. Not since he'd been discharged. But she wanted to. His arm tightened against her, but something was missing.

"Matt?"

"Hm?"

"What happened to your arm?"

His fucking arm.

Why the hell did it always come back to that one damn thing?

"They didn't much care for a man with a hook for a hand."

The prosthetic was gone, leaving him with a stump just below his elbow that was abso-fucking-lutely useless. About as much good as he was to her now, but when one of the kids at the orphanage came running in screaming about two men pushing Emery into a boat, he'd gone ballistic.

"What are they going to do to us?" Emery's voice was so small, so broken it hurt him. His sister, Sarah, and Emery were the literal definition of joy and happiness. People like them needed protecting, but a whole platoon of men might not be enough.

"They're traffickers, and not the good kind. We're Americans, near the border. They probably know they won't be able to sell us, so they'll kill me if I'm lucky and..." He couldn't say it. He couldn't put Emery and brutality in the same sentence.

She shuddered and held on to him tighter. He'd give the rest of his left arm for this to be happening at home, or even the hotel. Emery clutching his shoulders, the little sounds she would make in pleasure. Blood rushed to his cock. Of all the times for him to get wood, this was the worst.

Lightning lit up the sky followed by a crack of thunder. Their clothes were soaked and coated with mud and grime.

"If I'm lucky they'll what? Kill me too?"

She wasn't that naïve. Emery worked all over the world on humanitarian projects and regularly went to dangerous areas. They'd thought it was safe in Mukdahan.

"Yeah," he lied.

"No one's going to come after us?"

"They will, but it'll be too late." He rested his chin on top of her head. If it weren't for the mud, she'd smell of jasmine.

Some hero he was. There was little to no chance of her coming back alive, so he'd gone after her. He wasn't much use anymore. Why would he have thought he could save the damsel in distress?

They sat in the rain and the mud, clinging to each other. Every so often a bolt of lightning would flash and Emery would flinch and squeeze him a bit tighter. It was probably a good thing he didn't have another hand. He might not stop himself from touching her. Brush his fingers through her spun gold hair.

"I had a crush on you in high school," Emery said quietly.

One moment then two slipped by. Had he dreamed those words?

"You were pretty cute back then." Hell, she'd been the material of boot camp jerk-off sessions in a fucking cheerleader uniform. She'd been so excited about making head cheerleader, and all he could think about was her giving head.

"So why didn't you ask me out?" She tipped her head back and stared up at him.

He shifted a little. "I was six years older. That would've gotten me into some serious trouble."

"Not with me."

"Why are you telling me this now?"

"If I'm going to die I might as well ask. I'm cold." Her teeth were chattering like a jackhammer; the fear and weather weren't helping her either.

"Come here. Sit on my lap. It'll get you out of the water at least."

Emery slid across his thighs. Her clothes were caked with mud, and she was ice cold. She settled against his chest, and he tucked her under his coat. He wasn't afraid of death—they were old pals—but he didn't want this for Emery. He had to think of something to get them out.

"You okay?" he asked.

Mud streaked her cheeks, tendrils of hair were slicked to her brow, and even in the near-darkness he could see the bump on the side of her head. She was still beautiful, wild and crazy, sweet and tender. She'd driven him crazy over the years. He hated that this might be the way she saw him last. A washed-up SEAL with nothing to offer her. Not even an escape plan.

Emery wiped away some of the mud caked on Matt's face. If she got the rest off would there be a suit of armor under there?

She appreciated him telling her the worst-case scenario, but she didn't believe their options had run out. There was always hope so long as they were breathing.

If this was it, she didn't want to spend her last hours being scared. Not when Matt was there. She couldn't read him, but she refused to allow his stern stare to cow her. She might not know much about the man he'd become, but she recognized that core of strength he'd always had.

She rested her forehead against his and dropped her gaze to his mouth. He had great lips for a guy. The last time she'd been this close to him, she'd been afraid of kissing him. Now she knew what real fear was.

Matt held still as she closed the distance between them. The instant her lips touched his everything else faded away. His arm around her shoulders tightened, plastering her against his chest. She cupped his cheek and opened for him. His tongue thrust into her mouth. His stubble rasped against her and she melted. Heat blossomed in her chest and spread through her body. The reality of kissing him was better than anything she'd dreamed.

A peel of thunder startled her into sitting bolt upright, gasping for breath and dizzy.

"It's just thunder," Matt murmured against her neck.

They were in a pit, and there were people out there who might decide killing them was less bother than feeding them. Her desire withered, and she collapsed back against his chest.

He cradled her close, offering no false words of comfort.

She wrapped her arms around his shoulders and buried her face in the crook of his neck. "I should have kissed you a long time ago."

A bolt of lightning flashed so near she smelt ozone. Sparks flew overhead and someone screamed. Her heart jumped. Any moment they were going to come for her.

Matt stood, dragging her to her feet.

"What are you doing?" Her feet were so numb she stumbled and Matt had to steady her.

He pressed his back against the far side of the pit and dragged in a deep breath through his nostrils. "Do you smell that? The building caught on fire. Which side flips up?"

"What?" She lifted up on her toes, but couldn't see anything.

"Which side, Emery?"

"That side."

His gaze bored into hers. "This might be the only chance we get. I can't climb up with one hand. I need you to give me a boost, and then I can pull you out."

"Okay." She nodded and crossed to the other side. Emery made a cup with her hands. She didn't know how she would boost him up, but she'd try anything. "Like this?"

"On three. One. Two. Three." He took one stride, the mud and water slurping around his boots and planted his foot into her grasp.

She grunted and slammed back into the wall of the pit. Her hands slipped. Matt grunted, but had a grip on something.

"I can't get up." He swung a little from side to side.

"Use my back." She leaned forward and braced her hands on her knees. Matt kicked her in the ass and the heel of his boots bit into her back. "Oh god, hurry." She groaned and tried to ignore the toe to the kidney.

Matt hoisted himself up and shimmied through a weak spot between the bamboo poles. His legs disappeared. Emery stared up in disbelief. Had he really just escaped? Rain still fell at a steady pace, making her blink rapidly. Smoke and light bathed the sky over head. Something wasn't just on fire, it was blazing.

Someone grunted and for the longest minutes of her life, she didn't see or hear Matt.

"Matt?" she whispered.

Still no answer. She tried and failed to find some sort of handhold, but the ground was too wet and crumbled under her grasp. What if something had happened to Matt?

"Give me your hand."

Her head snapped up.

Matt lay on his stomach above her, his good arm extended toward her. She could have cried with relief. "I don't know if I can jump that high." Still, she backed up a pace.

"You can do it."

She jumped as high as she could, and fell short of the mark.

"Try it again. Come on."

She backed up again. "Go without me."

"Don't you fucking say that. I'll crawl back in there with you before I leave you."

Emery crouched and tried to jump straight up, but her sneakers had sunk too far into the mud, and she pitched forward onto her knees.

"Again, Emery. Now. Come on."

"I can't," she sobbed. She wasn't strong or fast like Matt. Even with one arm he could do more.

"You can. Get rid of the shoes. Jump on top of them."

She slipped out of the waterlogged shoes and jumped again. Matt wrapped his hand around her wrist, and she dangled there for a moment. She could hear his grunting and felt his grip slip the smallest bit.

"Hold on to me," he got out between clenched teeth.

She grasped his wrist with her other hand and slowly, inch by inch, he pulled her up. She grabbed the poles and helped him lift her. Rain still pounded them, but from ground level, it didn't seem so bad.

The body of a man, the one who had sneered at her, lay a few feet away, and beyond him at least a dozen people were running around a house built on stilts.

"Don't look. Come on." Matt urged her to her feet and half carried her. They plunged into what looked like a wild jungle.

"Where are we going?" she gasped. Her feet hurt from the cold, rocks underfoot, and god only knew what else.

"I hot-wired a truck and left it about half a mile away. Do I need to carry you?"

Yes, she needed very much to be carried far, far away.

"No," she managed to get out between panting for breath. Any second those men were going to chase them down.

Matt stopped her in her tracks. "Look at me."

She lifted her chin and stared into his eyes.

"Nothing bad will happen to you. I promise."

Her breath caught in her throat. "And promises are for keeping."

He kissed her lips so quickly it might not have happened, and then dragged her further into no-man's-land.

Matt stood outside of the hotel room in the same spot he'd been in for five minutes. The last thirty-six hours were a blur. The pit. Dashing through the jungle. Stealing a boat to cross to Thailand and being caught mid-river by border patrol. There were a thousand instances where they could've died, and here he was, back in Thailand.

The door cracked open.

"Just wanted to make sure you're okay," he blurted. Had he knocked?

"You've been standing there forever. Come in." Emery swung open.

He stepped over the threshold even though he knew he shouldn't. She was safe. She didn't need him anymore.

"Where's Sarah?" He'd expected his sister to stick to her like glue.

Emery closed the door and flipped the locks. How badly had this episode scarred her? She hugged an old, threadbare robe around herself.

"I couldn't take her staring at me like I was a ghost." She glanced at the balcony doors. He hadn't missed the chair and traveling crates stacked in front of the glass.

He opened his mouth to tell her it would pass, the nightmares would go away and she would stop looking over her shoulder, but they were lies.

"Stay with me? Please?" She stared at a point over his shoulder. The goose egg had gone down, and she'd scrubbed clean, but the real marks weren't visible to the naked eye.

"Whatever you want."

Emery walked straight into him and wrapped her arms around his waist. She took a deep, shuddering breath and released it. "I only feel safe when I can see you."

A lump formed in his throat. The whole mission there and back had been dumb luck. He patted her shoulder. "I'm right here."

They stood there for several, long moments until Emery relaxed. She peeked up at him and damn if he didn't want to kiss her again. He'd kissed plenty of women, but no one else had ever made him want like she had. Emery made him think of home and rumpled sheets.

"I'll sit in that chair if you want to try to sleep," he offered. Yeah, he was a creep, but watching over her would at least make him feel useful.

Emery shook her head and stepped away. Of course she

wouldn't need him. She was a strong woman.

"I want you in bed with me." She untied the belt on her robe, and he almost swallowed his tongue. She wore panties and a T-shirt so thin he could see the hard tips of her breasts. Sexier than any fancy lingerie he'd ever seen.

"Emery, you don't know what you're saying." He tried to close her robe, save himself from the visual he'd hoard the rest of his life, but she pushed his hand aside.

"No, I've been half in love with you all my life, and it's stupid to not do anything about it." She shoved the robe off her shoulders and reached for him, sliding her hands under his shirt and up his back. "You could have died last year. We could have died yesterday. It made me realize I don't want to wait anymore. Especially when it comes to you."

She pushed his shirt up and gave him a little glare.

Matt lifted his eyes to the ceiling, damning himself for being weak, and then pulled it off. She was already tabbing his jeans open and shoving the last of his clothing off. He kicked out of his shoes and stood there, naked as the day he was born.

Emery stepped back, her eyes flicking over the scars and burn marks from the IED shrapnel that had taken his arm. He had other prosthetics in his room, but he'd come to her without even one. Just him. But was that enough? She deserved to be swept off her feet. He couldn't give her everything, but he could give her this.

Matt wrapped his arm around her waist and she hopped up, wrapping her legs around his hips and clinging to him. She pressed her mouth to his, suckling his lower lip between hers. He thrust his tongue into her mouth, hungry for more.

He laid her down on the bed and rolled them until she was on top.

Emery sat up and smiled at him. It was the simplest gesture, but it stole his breath. She was so damn gorgeous. Slowly, she stripped her shirt off, revealing inch by slow inch of smooth creamy skin. He'd wondered what color her nipples would be, and now he knew they were pink like cotton candy.

Candy he wanted to taste.

He sat up and pulled her closer, dipping his head to take one of her tight peaks into his mouth. Her nails dug tracks into his shoulder. He wanted another hand to touch her, but all he had was a damn stump.

Her hand trailed down his mangled arm, over the ugly scars and back up. He held still, waiting for her to wake up and realize her mistake.

"You're the strongest man I know." Her gaze bored into his.

The reverent awe smacked him in the gut.

"I'm no one special. Just another Captain Hook."

That made her lips quirk up. "You're more than that."

Emery pushed his shoulders back. He didn't want to give her space, he wanted to hold on to her for as long as she'd let him, but in the end he lay back on the mattress.

"I've thought about this a lot." Her cheeks sported a rosy blush.

"Me too." And reality was better than any dream.

Her gaze dropped to his cock, and she licked her lips. She lowered to her elbows and peeked through her lashes as she grasped his hard length and kissed the mushroom cap. She opened her mouth and fuck all if it wasn't better than his fantasies. Her hair brushed his thighs as she sucked his cock, slowly working him in and out of her mouth.

It felt so good. He lifted his hips, silently begging for more, and she gave it to him as selflessly as she did everything.

He didn't deserve this, but he wanted it. He wanted her and everything she'd give him.

* * *

Emery sat back on her knees and pushed her panties off.

"Matt, I want you now." Could he see how much she wanted him?

She crawled up his body, hungry for him. Maybe it was intensified because of what they'd been through together, but she'd wanted him since before he was the war hero, since before he'd been the high-school football star.

He rolled them again until he was on top, pressing her down into the mattress.

She reached between them and ran her hand up his hard length, squeezing just enough to make him groan. She guided him to her entrance and he thrust. She gasped as he stretched her; it'd been so long since she'd been intimate with anyone. He thrust again, and her eyes rolled back. She lifted her hips. "Matt," she moaned and arched her back.

He thrust again, and she could feel all of him, the way he filled her, how he held her exactly where he wanted her. She lifted up for a kiss and he gave it to her, branding her with the heat boiling between them. He withdrew and thrust. Again and again. She was mesmerized by the look of sheer pleasure on his face, the way his head tilted back just a little as he watched her. She felt as though he could see straight to her soul.

"You're so fucking beautiful."

She reached between them, caressing the ladder of muscles crawling down his stomach and lower. Her fingers brushed his cock as he pumped in and out. She flicked her fingers over her clit, and her lips parted on a long moan. Her inner muscles clamped down, as he continued to piston in and out. Her spine arched, and she dug her fingers into his back and squeezed her thighs around his waist.

Emery wanted to tell Matt how much she loved him, but

it was too soon. Instead she bit her lip as ripples of pleasure coursed through her body, and held his gaze.

He groaned and his cock pulsed inside of her, spilling his seed until he was spent. It might have been her imagination, but she felt in tune with him. Could he love her in return?

Matt sagged, and she hugged him closer, not ready to let go. Dampness bathed her thighs. Of course, they hadn't remembered to use protection. The idea didn't send her into panic. If they had a child, would it have his eyes and her hair? Her heart skipped a beat at the thought of starting the family she'd always wanted with him.

He rolled to his side, taking her with him and flipping the comforter over them.

Emery snuggled close to Matt, unwilling to leave the warm cocoon of blankets. She never wanted to be cold again.

"Fuck." Matt sat straight up.

"I think that's your favorite word." She pried one eye open.

Matt turned toward her, his gaze wild with a different kind of panic.

"What's wrong?" She glanced at the door and the patio.

"We didn't use a condom. Could you get pregnant?" he asked, rubbing the side of his face.

She sat up and leaned on her knees. "Maybe. If I am, so what? I've always wanted kids. I don't want to wait anymore. If you don't want kids and I am pregnant, I'll work it out."

He turned to her, his gaze fierce. "I would never leave one of my own. I would never leave you."

She tugged him back down to the mattress, warmth and hope twining together in her chest. "I lied when I said I was half in love with you. I'm madly, head over heels for you."

Pain flashed across his face before he hid it behind that stony mask he'd gotten so good at showing people. "You should have someone able-bodied."

"Able-bodied?" She peeked under the blanket. "I think your body is able enough."

"That's not what I meant." He twirled a lock of her hair around his finger. The lines around his mouth and across his brow relaxed. "Kids, huh?"

Heat crawled up her neck. Telling herself to take no excuses for what she wanted was a lot easier in her head.

"I told myself before this last tour when I came home, if you were single, I was going to stop dragging my feet and ask you out. But I'm not the same man you knew. I've changed, and it's not all good—"

She cupped his face. He'd followed her, fought for her and rescued her. She didn't deserve him. "I don't care. I know how I feel."

His blue eyes glared. "Will you stop fucking interrupting me?"

"Sorry," she murmured, but couldn't help letting a smile steal across her lips because she thought she knew what he was having trouble saying. She waited, happiness blossoming inside her chest.

He pursed his lips, but there was a slight upturn in the corners. "I'm trying to say...I think I love you."

BIG GUNS

Michael Bracken

When the economy's in the toilet, you take any job you can get. The best I could find after the auto plant shut down required wearing an industrial-strength pushup bra under a white tee, skintight, too-short shorts that gave me a pronounced camel toe, and involved pouring cheap bourbon out of top-shelf bottles into dirty glasses I foisted on the barflies at Lucky's Corner Tavern. I missed dressing for the office, wearing skirt suits, blouses made of anything other than cotton, and bras that supported my breasts instead of trying to push them into my chin. I also missed my dignity, but most days it seemed a small price to pay to keep my creditors mollified. After all, I knew former coworkers who had exhausted their unemployment benefits and still hadn't found work of any kind.

Barflies weren't the only customers at Lucky's. A drug dealer and his muscled-up posse had taken up semipermanent residence in the back corner where they could watch the front and rear entrances while they conducted business with a steady stream of twitchy, lowlife street-level dealers.

Lucky Jr., the second-generation owner of the corner tavern, paid them no never mind so long as the drug dealer's clientele didn't bother his rummies. His attitude might just have been the posturing of an old man, because the illegal sawed-off shotgun he kept under the counter near the cash register might frighten some punk stick-up man brandishing a Saturday Night Special, but was insufficient against the overwhelming firepower of several fully automatic assault rifles.

I did my best to ignore the business transacted in the back corner of the bar and the men who conducted it, but one of the drug dealer's muscled-up posse members caught my eye every time he walked in. Often dressed in a tight-fitting black T-shirt, faded button-fly Levi's, and black lace-up work boots, he stood well over six feet tall, with broad shoulders and a thick chest that tapered down to a tight abdomen, firm ass, and thighs like tree trunks. The prominent bulge in the crotch of his jeans convinced me his thighs weren't the only parts of him with redwood-like qualities, and his greasy, shoulder-length black hair and failure to shave on any kind of consistent schedule only enhanced his thuggish appearance. His associates called him Howitzer—often shortened to Howie—because of his big guns, biceps as big as my thighs.

Even though he was exactly the sort of man I avoided, just seeing Howie swagger into the bar was enough to make me wet with desire, and I snuck surreptitious glances at him throughout my shift. I caught him eyeing me several times, but no more often than the other men in the bar. After all, despite how much I disliked my required apparel, I dressed to draw attention, increase alcohol sales and earn extra tips.

No drugs ever changed hands inside the bar. The dealer who

camped out in the back corner supplied the street-level dealers, who visited him to pay their bills and their respects but picked up their supplies elsewhere. On any given night several thousand dollars—potentially nearing a hundred thousand—might be in play in the back corner, and the dealer's posse was there to protect it.

I'd been working at the bar for more than a month before Howie ever spoke to me. One of the street-level dealers—a wiry little man whose eyes bounced left to right as if he were unable to focus—aggressively hit on me, suggesting in rather crude language what he wanted to stick in my mouth and what he expected me to do to it.

When I attempted to blow him off with a laugh and an equally crude comment about the probable size of his equipment, he reached across the bar and grabbed my arm, sinking sharp fingernails into my soft skin. I tried to pull away but his grip was too strong, and he pulled me tight against my side of the bar. I glanced to my left and realized I was too far from the cash register to grab the sawed-off.

By the time I returned my attention to the shifty-eyed man gripping my arm, Howie had left the back booth and had stepped behind him. He dropped his meaty fists on the man's shoulders and squeezed. "There a problem here?"

I glared at the man gripping my arm. "Is there?"

The shifty-eyed little man glanced over his shoulder at Howie. "No, I—"

He released his hold on my arm as Howie grabbed his belt with one hand and lifted him onto his toes. Howie spun him around and pointed him toward the door, making him walk on his tiptoes all the way there. He pushed the door open, planted one big black boot on the man's ass and shoved.

The door swung shut before I saw what happened to the

shifty-eyed drug dealer who had accosted me.

Howie returned to the bar. "Anybody ever gives you a problem like that," he said with a nod toward the door, "let me know and I'll take care of it for you."

"So now you're my self-appointed guardian angel?" I said, lifting my chin.

He stared into my eyes and lowered his voice so that only I could hear. "That's more accurate than you realize."

As I returned his gaze, Howie reached across the counter and gently touched my arm, his calloused fingertips brushing over the fingernail indentions left by the man who had accosted me. Unexpectedly, heat surged through my body, my heart began to race and my knees felt weak, exactly opposite of the reaction I'd had only a few minutes earlier when another man had touched me.

I knew I should pull away, but I didn't because I wanted Howie to feel the same rush of desire I felt, and I wanted him to pull me across the counter and smother me with kisses even though it went against everything I believed was right.

"You'd better put something on that," Howie said as he drew back his hand. "He broke the skin."

Maybe that's what finally pushed me over the edge. The thought that this big man, this thuggishly handsome man who existed only to protect and perpetuate a lifestyle that no self-respecting woman would ever find appealing, might be my Prince Charming, was so incongruous that it began to fuel my fantasies.

My love life had disappeared at the same time as my job at the auto plant, and the longer I went without, the more batteries I drained. During the next several months I often fantasized about Howie and how we might consummate our inappropriate fantasy relationship.

My favorite involved him taking me in the bar late at night after everyone had gone but the two of us.

Thinking I'm alone, I lock the front door and turn to see him coming from the men's room, buttoning his fly.

I lick my lips with the tip of my tongue. "You don't have to do that."

He leaves his belt undone and crosses the bar to where I stand. He pulls me into his arms, crushes my breasts between us and covers my mouth with his. His kiss is deep, firm, insistent and soon his tongue is buried in my mouth and I suck on it.

Howie reaches down, cups my ass with his big hands and lifts me off the floor. He carries me to the bar and sets me on the worn wood. Without a word, he strips off my tee, my bra, my shorts and my thong, tossing them aside. He settles onto a bar stool and hooks my legs over his shoulders. Then he kisses his way up the inside of my legs until his face is buried in the soft tangle of hair at the juncture of my thighs.

He draws his thick tongue along the length of it, and I am so wet with desire he stops to swallow not once but twice. As he licks me, his two-day-old beard growth scratches my thighs, the sandpaper-like roughness a sexy contrast to the silky smooth strokes of his tongue.

He drives his tongue into me and pulls back, quickly finding the tight bud of my clit. He teases it, licks it, licks around it and then draws it between his teeth and gently holds it as he spanks it with his tongue.

As I near orgasm, I grab two handfuls of his slicked-back black hair. My hips buck up and down, my eyelids flutter and then I cry out. He continues tonguing me but I've had enough. I push against his forehead, making him stop.

Howie isn't finished, though, and he lifts himself off the bar stool just enough to slide his jeans and underwear down to his knees. He pulls me off the bar and into his lap. The mushroom cap of his cock presses against my slick opening, and with only a slight readjustment, his cock penetrates me and I slide down its full length.

I lean back against the bar and hook my ankles behind Howie. He wraps one arm around my waist, places the other hand on my lower abdomen, his thumb pressed against my clit as he drives into me, and I come a second time before he erupts within me.

My fantasies remain only fantasies, because I would never allow myself to become involved with a man like the Howitzer, but the fantasies continue for several more weeks.

Then one Thursday night, a slow night for the bar but a busy night for the dealer in the back corner, something went wrong. I heard gunshots outside and the shifty-eyed street-level dealer who accosted me many months earlier burst into the bar followed by two other men, all of them armed.

The two legitimate customers in the bar scrambled for the exits and I dropped to the floor behind the bar. I heard gunfire so close it practically deafened me, but could see nothing of what was happening.

Then Howie dove over the bar and landed on top of me, pinning me to the floor with his weight. I had frequently fantasized about his hard body on top of me, but never like this.

"You'll be okay," he said, his gaze locking with mine, and his lips only a fraction of an inch from my mouth. "Everything will be okay. Just stay down."

He pushed himself off me, scrambled to the other end of the bar and shot a man who was running down the hall past the restrooms, headed toward the rear exit.

After a moment of silence, Howie eased out from behind the bar. I heard him moving around, and I slid quietly toward the cash register.

"You can get up now," he said. "It's over."

I rose with Lucky Jr.'s sawed-off shotgun in my hands. I saw the carnage of the attempted robbery, but did my best to ignore it.

"Not yet, it isn't," I told Howie. "Drop your gun and lift your hands."

After Howie did as instructed, I rested the shotgun's shortened barrel on the bar and used one hand to reach for the phone, intending to call the police. Before I had finished dialing, though, the bar was overrun with uniformed police, and I was instructed to drop the shotgun.

I spent the night at the police station answering questions, and I returned to work as soon as Lucky's Corner Tavern reopened. The bar did a booming business the night the police finished combing the crime scene, and Lucky Jr. recognized the bar's new appeal. He didn't bother patching the bullet holes. He raised prices on everything, and he even had to hire additional help to serve all the thrill-seekers who sought out the bar.

Two months after the shootout at Lucky's, at the end of a particularly busy Saturday night, I pushed the last customer out the door and was about to lock it when a big man in a blue pin-striped suit pushed the door open.

"I'm sorry," I said without looking up from the badge hanging from his belt, "we're closed."

"Even for me?"

When I recognized Howie's voice, I looked up into the big man's eyes. He was clean-shaven and his greasy, shoulder-length hair had been transformed into a crew cut. As my heart raced and heat rushed to my core, I realized my self-appointed guardian angel wasn't the dangerous low-life thug I had been imprudently lusting after for months, but was instead exactly the kind of man of which forever-after dreams are made. I pushed the door closed behind him and locked it.

Then Howie scooped me into his arms and lifted me from the floor. He kissed me—kissed me hard—and carried me across the room to set me on the bar.

"You don't know how often I've dreamed of exactly this," I murmured as he stripped off my tee.

And then Special Agent Howard Hardcastle made my dreams come true.

NATURAL APPETITES

Adele Dubois

Even at seventy miles per hour, Michael Kent spotted the woman on the roadside in serious trouble. He checked his mirrors and lifted his foot off the gas before crossing two lanes to enter the shoulder. He tapped the brakes, slowed to a stop and threw his transmission into reverse. The Mustang closed the gap to the haphazardly parked SUV in a blink.

The stranded woman waved her arms at him in frantic motions. Her mouth formed a perfect O as she issued screams he couldn't hear above the traffic noise or the sound of his tires kicking up cinders.

As he opened his door, she appeared by his window, tears streaming down her face. She pointed to her car. "My son!"

Mickey went into full paramedic mode with the realization a medical emergency, and not a mechanical problem, waited in the SUV. He hurried to the woman's car and flung the rear door open.

Not good. The kid, who couldn't have been older than seven,

was already turning blue as he struggled for breath.

"I called nine-one-one," the mother cried. "But he needs help *now!*"

Mickey couldn't have agreed more. He unbuckled the boy's seat belt and laid him supine on the backseat before clearing his mouth and starting chest compressions. He spoke to the woman over his shoulder. "Tell me what happened."

"We were driving home from a birthday party. Jack was playing with the things inside his party bag. He ate some candy and then blew up a balloon. Suddenly, he started thrashing his legs and making gagging sounds. I pulled over as fast as I could, but didn't know what was wrong. I called emergency services when nothing I did helped." Her dark eyes pleaded. "Can you help him?"

"I'm a paramedic. I'll do everything I can." He told the woman his name. "I'm with Appleton Fire Station."

The mother released a shaky sigh of relief. Her body trembled. "Thank god!"

Mickey's brain processed the information the woman gave him. Candy. Food allergy? Gagging. Choking.

Balloon.

"Where's the balloon?"

The mother dumped the party bag on the floorboard. "I don't see it."

Jesus. Mickey felt for the penknife in his back pocket. He had about thirty seconds to decide whether or not to do a tracheotomy on the kid. "Any straws inside the car? I need one. Now! Go!"

The Heimlich maneuver didn't typically work with balloons, but now that he knew what he was dealing with, he decided to try to clear the child's airway before taking more drastic action. He tilted the boy's head back, opened his mouth and reached into his throat while depressing the tongue with his thumb. There. The tips of his fingers touched something pliable.

Mickey had become some kind of cosmic disaster magnet since Iraq. His fate had been sealed the day a soldier died in his arms while Saddam's statue fell in central Baghdad. Since then, life or death situations found him wherever he went, on or off the clock. He no longer questioned why, just did his best to serve his community. Right now, that meant saving this kid.

Mickey turned the boy over and started the Heimlich. The maneuver wouldn't expel the balloon, but might dislodge it enough to manually pull it free.

He pressed in and up on the child's solar plexus, hard enough to force the balloon to shift, but gently enough not to break Jack's ribs. If this didn't work, he'd have to do the trach. The child's color had turned from pale blue to dark. There were only seconds left.

Mickey turned the boy over again on the backseat. He reached into his throat, whispered a prayer when he pinched latex, and pulled.

The balloon slipped free and an enormous inhalation followed. Jack's eyes flew open and his jaw dropped as he gulped down autumn evening air. The child's color instantly improved. His mother crawled onto the backseat and took her son into her arms, soothing him as he began to wail.

Crying was good. The kid would take in plenty of oxygen.

Mickey stepped out of the car. "You need to take Jack to the nearest emergency room and have him checked out." He pulled his cell phone from his jacket pocket. "I'll call ahead and let them know you're coming." All Pennsylvania hospitals within a twenty-five mile radius were listed on his speed dial.

The sounds of sirens proceeded flashing lights, as a medical team pulled up behind the SUV, followed by a police cruiser.

Mickey closed his cell phone. "These guys will take it from here, ma'am."

He recognized the crew of EMTs and their paramedic from a neighboring town, and they nodded to him in return. They were almost as good as his Appleton team and would take proper care of the kid. Mickey leaned over and whispered in the other paramedic's ear. "Where the fuck were you guys?"

The other man released a weary sigh. "Car crash. Six victims. Elevator accident before that. It's been a crazy day."

Mickey slapped his counterpart on the back. "I hear you." Mickey's week included a heart attack, a stroke victim, a girl who fell from a third-story window, five car accidents and a supermarket trip and fall. Since most communities hired only one or two paramedics, with as many ambulances to serve them, their expertise was stretched thin.

Mickey headed toward his Mustang as the EMTs loaded the boy onto a stretcher. Before he got halfway to his car, footfalls sounded behind him. "Wait!"

He turned and Jack's mother threw herself into his arms. She hugged him tight. "My husband and I will never be able to thank you enough." After she released him, she kissed his cheek, and then pressed something into his palm. "Come to our place whenever you want. Where you're concerned, everything on the menu remains on the house."

Mickey glanced at the business card advertising an organic foods restaurant owned by *Your hosts, Andy and Elena* and suppressed a groan. These people were probably vegetarians at best and vegans at worst. He liked big, juicy cheeseburgers heaped with crisp bacon, or a Texas-sized steak piled high with fried onions and mushrooms. To maintain his muscle mass after daily workouts at the gym, he needed large quantities of protein.

He smiled at the woman. "Thanks."

They parted, and Mickey glanced at the time on his dashboard as he slid behind the wheel of his car. "Shit." He'd missed his after-work drinks date with Madelaine. Again. He checked his cell. No messages. His spoiled, over-sexed girlfriend had warned if he was late *one more time*, she'd be done with him. With her looks, men offered to crawl through glass to sleep with her. She'd made it clear Mickey could be easily replaced. One stiff cock was as good as another, as far as she was concerned. It would take her all of about five minutes to finish sulking and find a new guy. Maybe two, in ten.

He called her anyway, but Madelaine refused to answer. Mickey swore. He'd miss the luscious mouth that drank him in, slow and steady, like velvet whiskey. And her ass. He'd surely miss that.

His cell phone went dark.

Without a shadow of doubt, Mickey knew he'd just been dumped.

Mickey hadn't intended to stop by Andy and Elena's Organics Fantastic restaurant for dinner, but Elena had called the stationhouse three times since the incident on the roadside, and wouldn't take no for an answer. When he assured her she owed him nothing, she replied, "My chef will make something extra special for you," and hung up.

The eatery was located on the outskirts of Appleton, less than six miles from the fire station. He decided to take his bean sprouts on sandpaper bread, and drink his broccoli-and-beets soy shake like a man, and be finished with his obligation to this family.

Mickey expected to find minimal clientele seated at unvarnished bamboo tables and chairs inside a stark room bearing

grass floor mats when he stepped through the doors of Organics
Fantastic. Instead, glowing candles warmed the rooms of a
restored farmhouse, filled with well-dressed people seated in
plush chairs at polished mahogany tables. Original artwork
hung on freshly painted walls. Expensive wool carpeting cushioned his feet as he made his way to the pretty blonde hostess,
who smiled in welcome.

The appreciative glint in her eyes made him grateful he'd
worn business casual for dinner instead of his usual T-shirt and
jeans. When he introduced himself, the hostess replied, "We've
been expecting you, Mr. Kent. I'll tell the owners you're here."
She led him to a reserved table in a private corner of the main
room.

Elena hurried to Mickey's side moments later, hugged him
and introduced her husband, Andy. The men shook hands
and chatted like old friends before Andy disappeared into the
bar. He returned with a set of glasses and a bottle of the finest
scotch whiskey, poured Mickey a drink and left the bottle on
the table.

Mickey took a grateful swallow and looked around the
impressive room. A tall, handsome waitress brought him a
menu. When he opened the cover, he couldn't have been more
surprised by its contents. Grass-fed beef. Free-range chicken.
Coldwater shrimp and lobster. There wasn't a glass of soy milk
or a bean sprout to be found.

He salivated and licked his lips before taking another
mouthful of scotch. At the smooth, heavenly taste, he closed his
eyes and sighed.

"Glad to see you're enjoying our little part of the world,"
said a soothing feminine voice, adding a layer of comfort to his
reverie.

Mickey nodded and opened his eyes. The poised young

woman standing before him lit his senses like a lightning strike.

She might have been twenty-two to his twenty-nine, but not much more. Everything about her looked glossy, supple and smooth. From the frank, dark eyes and shining black hair that touched her shoulders in waves, to the ample curves of her breasts and hips, this woman looked the epitome of health and vitality. He blinked, stunned by her heady effect on his system.

She smiled, and clean white teeth behind lush red lips rushed blood to his groin. Visions of her mouth on him, everywhere and all at once, filled his head. Her beauty warmed him from the inside out, like the spirits he'd consumed. The sight of her intoxicated him and almost made him drop the glass he held.

"I'm Amanda. I wanted to meet the man who saved Jack's life before I cooked for you."

Mickey reached for an empty glass and poured her a drink, steadying his hand over the lip. "Join me." He set the tumbler on the table and pulled a chair closer to his. Then he stood and held the chair out for her while she took the seat beside him.

He wanted to press his thigh against hers through her gauzy red skirt, but resisted the primal urges she stirred in him. Good manners demanded restraint, though he wanted nothing more than to kiss her senseless, tear the clothes from her voluptuous figure and make love to her on the tabletop in full view of the others. The natural heat from her body wafted over his, merging the pheromones raging between them.

He stared into her eyes and saw she felt it too. Instant chemistry. Connection. An attraction so rare it turned kinetic on contact.

Some called it love at first sight.

Amanda. Even her name sounded beautiful.

"I never met a hero before. That's what you are, you know."

Her dark lashes lowered and lifted, and she smiled at him with admiration.

Mickey shook his head. "I hate to disappoint you, but I only did what I'm trained to do."

She made sounds of disagreement. "Elena told me at least a hundred and fifty cars passed her on the highway and ignored her pleas for help. Of all those people, don't you think *one* might have been medically trained? Or at least cared enough to respond to her cries? No. You stopped. Only you." Amanda touched her glass of scotch to his in a silent toast.

Mickey took her hand in his and she let him hold it. He wanted to learn everything he could about Amanda and this place. Organics Fantastic, indeed. "Nothing here is what I expected." He squeezed her fingers before letting go.

She smiled and threw her head back with a knowing laugh, understanding his inference. "*Organic* means untouched by artificiality. Consumed in its natural state. We eat only healthy foods unspoiled by chemicals, preservatives, hormones, steroids and genetically modified seeds or cells. Pure."

Pure. Mickey gazed at the stunning woman by his side and knew that was true for her too. The satin white skin of her face and arms looked smooth as cream. Her skin looked supple and welcoming to the touch. He longed to run his hands along her generous thighs, imagining sleek roads leading to heaven between her legs.

His cock hardened beneath the table so quickly and completely it took his breath. This woman had turned him wild. Blood rushed to his face and phallus in equal measure. He poured another drink as a distraction, before he lost control and embarrassed them both.

Why had he ever thought women like Madelaine, vain and weightless, with aesthetically enhanced breasts and protruding collarbones, looked sexy? Why had he accepted her endless diets and liquid fasts as a normal way to live? Was it because his generous muscle mass seemed larger and stronger compared to her leanness? Or had he been brainwashed to believe gaunt women were more desirable?

His rounded muscles and tight angles blended with the curves and planes of Amanda's lush body like yin and yang. He met her eyes again and read passion and longing in their depths. This was a woman of consequence. Of substance.

He sensed she wouldn't refuse him if he gave himself to her honestly and completely. A woman like Amanda would nurture and heal. She could chase away his demons with a kiss.

With that final thought, he leaned into her and took her mouth with his. The kiss became his first impulsive act since turning away from his partner in Iraq, distracted by the fall of Saddam's statue, seconds before a bomb exploded. That was the unretractable moment that changed his life, all those years ago.

Amanda tasted like fine whiskey and raspberry lip-gloss, freedom and forgiveness. When her tongue touched his and her hand caressed his cheek to bring him closer, he melted into her.

Mickey had kissed many women in his life, but none had radiated the warmth and promise of this woman. Rather than take from him, she gave. Despite his advances, she offered. The generosity of her response to his demand touched his soul.

He knew in that moment he'd do anything to win her.

When they broke the kiss, Amanda's expression looked as amazed as Mickey felt. Yet a smile touched her mouth, and a sigh like contentment escaped her lips as she sat back in her chair.

Mickey said nothing but watched her recompose. Amanda smoothed the fabric of her skirt and ran a hand over the bodice of her blouse. After a moment, she glanced at him from the corners of her eyes. "I want to cook for you now."

Mickey reached out to touch her forearm. "Should I be sorry I did that?"

She lifted her gaze to his and shook her head. "If you were sorry, it would mean the kiss meant nothing."

His hand closed on her arm. "You feel it too?"

Amanda lowered her lids and nodded. She laid a hand over his. "I'm not sure what to do with this chemistry between us. I thought instant attraction only happened in stories. I need to sort things out while I make the best meal you've ever tasted."

Amanda Greer pulled her best stainless-steel pots and pans from their hooks above the stove and began to create Mickey Kent's dinner. She chased the kitchen staff out of her way while she pan-seared steak, caramelized onions, and steamed vegetables using distilled water and real organic butter.

The chocolate cake she'd baked from scratch cooled on a sideboard. When Mickey was ready for dessert, she'd spread homemade chocolate icing over its thick layers and then make espresso. She'd cut two thick slices, pour two cups of coffee, and sit with Mickey at the table. Andy and Elena would join them for after-dinner brandy.

When her boss told her about the handsome paramedic with penetrating blue eyes and sand-colored hair who saved Jack's life, Amanda had been anxious to meet him. Her motive then had been to offer thanks with the finest meal she could create. The stranger had rescued not only a child and his family, but Amanda, as well.

Jack's death would have destroyed his parents and their business. If Amanda lost her way of life to tragedy and devastation, where would she go? After losing her apartment in a Colorado wildfire and resettling in Pennsylvania, she wanted to put down roots. Appleton suited her. Rich with agriculture and open space, here she'd instantly felt at home. She'd grown fond of Andy, Elena and Jack, and the community too. They were like extended family. Mickey Kent had saved the hearts and spirits of many people by his intervention. Maybe that's why she'd fallen a little in love with him before they met.

While the steak sizzled, Amanda warmed Mickey's plate and checked the vegetables for proper tenderness. She pulled fresh-baked bread from the oven, and its delectable scent filled the air. Her mouth watered. This meal must be perfect. Though her original motive for cooking had been gratitude, that had changed with a single impulsive kiss.

Mickey's entrance into her life proved she could trust the outcome of the unexpected. He put ego aside for the sake of others and took a risk with her by exposing his feelings. Through food art, Amanda wanted to share an intimate part of herself to bring them closer.

Her lips still tingled in response to his. The throbbing between her legs beat gentle reminders that the most desirable man she'd ever met waited outside her kitchen. Her arms ached to hold him, and her belly tightened at thoughts of them moving naked together.

Mickey Kent had unleashed the woman in her.

When the time was right, Amanda would act on her feminine impulses. For now, she would feed him. She sensed that making love with Mickey would be as natural and nourishing as the wholesome foods that filled them.

Mickey sat back in his chair a week later at Organics Fantastic, just before closing time, and groaned with satisfaction. "You're a genius, Amanda. That chicken breast with wild mushrooms was delicious."

Amanda smiled from her seat beside him. "That's how chickens taste when they're not shot up with steroids and hormones. All I did was roast yours with a little sauce and some artistic ingenuity."

"My grandmother used to cook meals like these. Are you sure you're not a nineteen-fifties throwback?"

"I'm told I have an old soul." Amanda grinned at him in the sexy way that made his heart and everything below his belt go thump. "As they say, everything old is new again."

He reached out and touched a shining tendril of her hair. "This will be my third and final visit here, unless I pay for my meal. I appreciate your hospitality, but I refuse to wear out my welcome." Mickey had taken things slow but steady with Amanda after their initial meeting, to see if their attraction held or burned itself out.

He'd never wanted her more.

Mickey called or texted Amanda all week to let her know he was thinking of her, and brought some of the guys from the stationhouse around for lunch to help Andy and Elena grow their business. The restaurant had been a hit with the crew and adopted as their watering hole. As a bonus, Mickey hadn't faced a single medical emergency inside the restaurant. He could relax here. His life blended with his newfound friends at Organics Fantastic, and he'd never been happier.

He brushed a hand over Amanda's shoulder, savoring the sensations of pliant skin beneath sleek cotton. He wanted to drag his hand to the fullness of her breast and knead its softness, or reach beneath her skirt to the source of her heat, but resisted the impulse. "Take a walk with me." He needed to be alone with this woman.

Amanda stood and urged him to follow. Mickey pulled his jacket from the chair beside him and Amanda lifted her sweater from the coat closet. Hand in hand, they stepped outside into the crisp autumn air.

"This way," Amanda whispered. She led him along the path stretching from the front porch to a stand of pines and oaks on the rear lawn, illuminated by lamplight and a bright harvest moon. When they reached the privacy of the trees, Mickey removed his jacket and wrapped it around her back. In one fluid motion, he pressed her torso against an ancient oak and kissed her.

Amanda wrapped her arms around his neck and kissed him back while her fingers stroked his hairline, raising goose bumps along his skin. His breathing turned heavy as she lowered her hands to his chest and ran her palms over his nipples and pectorals. Quickly, she unbuttoned his shirt and reached inside to pinch and caress him.

His head lolled back with the sensations her fingers created. Silken hands ran over his flesh and then worked his belt buckle. His erection strained beneath his pants zipper. Her mouth trailed hot kisses over his throat before her tongue lapped his chest. The knowledge that she wanted him sent his senses reeling. He wanted to do right by her.

Mickey lifted Amanda off her feet and pressed her back against the tree for support while she wrapped her legs around his waist. The short skirt she wore shifted above her hips. Mickey cupped her bottom and groaned with pleasure as his hands touched firm, naked skin. Amanda wore only a thong.

It took mere seconds for him to tear the fragile fabric and toss it to the ground. He stared down at the most beautiful pussy he'd ever seen, or would ever see again, spread wide and waiting for him. Using his thumb, he ran circles around her clitoris until Amanda shuddered.

Then Mickey released the fly of his khakis.

Amanda had gone out of her mind with desire for Mickey. Was this what crazy in love meant? That offering yourself, body and soul, to another seemed the most natural thing to do?

She rested the crown of her head against the oak tree. Her back remained cushioned by Mickey's jacket and her sweater, and his waist supported her legs, while he suckled her nipples and stroked her breasts as if he were a starving man.

While he pinched the sensitive areolae and plump flesh, the length of his cock slid over her slick folds in a steady rhythm. The underside of the wide head rubbed her swollen clitoris until the pressure inside her built to near bursting. Pleasure rode over her in waves, and she cried out in anticipation of her climax.

"I want to make love to you," he said against her ear, his breaths coming in rapid pants. "Let me fuck you."

Amanda clutched his hips tighter against hers, lifting and sliding her clit along the thick length of his shaft. Her slick juices made the motions easy. "I want that too."

He released her and set her feet on the ground. Then Mickey took his jacket and spread it over the grass. Holding her hands, he guided her to the makeshift bed. Amanda lay under the bright fall moon and slid off her skirt in anticipation.

The crackle of cellophane preceded Mickey's return to her. He spread her legs, lifted her hips and lay between her thighs.

Instead of penetrating her as she expected, he lowered his mouth to her vulva and licked the tender skin in quick, erotic strokes. She cried out with pleasure unlike any other she'd known, and then covered her mouth, for fear the others inside the farmhouse would hear her.

No man had ever done this for her. She'd let men touch her and she'd had orgasms by their hands or hers, but no one had ever licked her clit or slid his tongue inside her channel.

"I'm so close," she warned. She wanted to climax around him. Though she'd never had intercourse, fingers had stretched and teased her. She knew enough about her sexuality to measure her responses.

Mickey lifted himself over her body and guided the tip of his sheathed cock into the opening of her pussy. "I'll try not to hurt you," he whispered.

"I know," she replied, and meant it.

He circled the head against her rim for maximum lubrication and then pushed inside, just a bit.

She inhaled audibly, though not from fear but bliss. Mickey brushed a hand over her cheek while he held himself upright with the other. "Are you ready?"

A husky reply escaped her throat. "Oh yeah."

Apparently, that was all the encouragement Mickey needed. He thrust into her again, harder this time, and then withdrew. He repeated the pattern until he met no resistance and she had taken in all of him. She lifted her hips to meet his tempo.

They swayed together until Amanda soared past her pain to her peak. When Mickey reached between her legs and rubbed the pad of his thumb over her clit while he fucked her, Amanda fell over the edge. When she climaxed, Mickey came too.

Mickey and Amanda arrived at Organics Fantastic for a special birthday celebration weeks later. Andy, Elena and the waitstaff set out lunch in the main dining area while children played games in another room under the watchful eyes of their parents.

The restaurant had been decorated with orange and yellow crepe paper streamers and a banner that read HAPPY 8TH

Birthday Jack in block lettering. An enormous cake, shaped like a train, took center stage.

Mickey eyed the decorations as he set their colorfully wrapped present on the gift table. "No balloons."

Amanda nodded. "They've been banned from the premises."

"Ah." Mickey wrapped an arm around Amanda's waist. "So, what do you think, gorgeous? Should we have two children or four after we get married?"

Amanda lifted on tiptoe to press a kiss against his cheek. "I need a proper proposal first. Then let's decide."

Mickey pulled her closer. "The sooner the better, my love."

SEAL DESTINY

Sharon Hamilton

S pecial Operator Chief Luke Paulsen had that dream again.
Her red lips pressed like tiny pillows against his cool mouth.
Though he was buried in his Afghan dugout bunk, he could feel
the delicate vibration of her moan as her lust for him whispered
things. Unmentionable things. No matter how hard he tried,
he couldn't recall her words. He could only remember the heat
washing over him as she breathed life into him. Again. Like she
did every night.

A sharp crack of gunfire forced him to open his eyes. He
caught a glimpse of Carson's scared face in profile just before the
young marine got the round in the chest that exited out between
his shoulder blades. In a graceful dance performed all too often,
Carson fell into his arms, and Luke watched the youngster's
life bleed out onto the sandy pit and all over his boots. He held
Carson's clear blue gaze, and, without saying a word, told him
he'd see him again one day. The boy's eyes remained open and
fixed after his soul had departed. Luke became witness to the

young marine's passage from his arms into the arms of death.

A split second later, Luke remembered who he was and why he was here. A day's ride by donkey from anywhere. He lifted the tiny mirror on a wire, the sun to his back.

Still clutching the body of the lifeless marine, he followed the trajectory of the round that had killed his young apprentice and caught the glint of dark blue steel disappearing into a blackened doorway. Laying the marine down gently, he picked up his H&K MP5, counted to five while he clicked the safety once. Before he saw the barrel of the insurgent's rifle again, he fired off several rounds that landed exactly ten inches above the protuberance and saw the red spray of a kill.

Was it wrong that the color of the spray reminded him of her crimson lips? That he died a thousand little deaths with each of her kisses?

His dreams were stealing his present.

A week later, SOC Luke watched the sun pour itself into the horizon on one of San Diego's white sand beaches. The afterglow felt good. So did the blush on his face from the three beers he'd finished. He usually drank with the rest of his SEAL Team III. But this last DT, Dissociative Tour, in Afghanistan had given him a cadre of young marines eager to prove themselves, along with Carson, the medic-in-training.

But Carson had drawn a different card and would be taking the short flight home. Luke raised his long-necked IPA to the sunset and toasted the man.

"To all the young hearts you won't break," he whispered to the soothing waves and the sunset.

It was a damned shame. He thought Carson would have made an excellent doctor.

Luke heard laughter as two lovelies in shorts ran past him to splash in the surf. Slender tanned legs kicked droplets of white foam into the air. He loved watching the girls' carefree spirit, just being goofy and lacking an ounce of self-consciousness. He couldn't help but smile.

The dark-haired one with the cutoff inside-out sweatshirt that showed her muscled midriff stopped and turned to face Luke. Her brown eyes were wide set. Her thin nose led to full lips that were stained bright red. She licked those lips and pushed her chocolate-brown hair from her forehead, exposing a delicious ridge of little lines on an otherwise smooth and flawless forehead. With a tiny angle she tilted her head to the side and waved in that embarrassed way her mother must have told her never to do. Especially to a strange sailor sitting alone on the beach with empty beer bottles at his feet.

Luke waved back, using the same three middle fingers she used, sending his communication off with a shy smile. He imitated the angle of her head and felt the dangerous curiosity and wonder of their chance meeting.

He wanted her in the worst way.

The blonde was pulling her friend, pleading, but she wasn't having any of it. Luke's unspoken message had touched her, and those golden tethers of his thoughts drew her to him, just as if he had special powers. It was lovely when that happened. He could almost believe in the supernatural, like those paranormal guys his sister read about in her romance novels.

The exquisite young thing with the well-defined legs came to within striking distance. If he wanted to, and hell yes he wanted to in the worst way, he could reach out and bring her to his arms and he could tell she wouldn't resist. But it would be so much better if he showed a little restraint.

Those who wait? What was that saying?

No matter. Luke felt the confusing enchantment like vamps

did in those books. It was a pleasant fantasy. Let her have her way with him. *Yes.* He could tell she felt she had a date with destiny.

I can be your destiny for one night, darlin'.

She disposed of her friend with a sharp command and, alone now, stepped closer to Luke. "You look like you could use some company," she said as she swung her upper torso from side to side.

Her feet had implanted themselves in the sand, and he watched her pink nail polish peek out between the grains.

Lady, you have lovely toes.

But, she'd asked a question that needed an answer. "That depends," he murmured, stunned at the joy it gave him to let his eyes walk slowly up her body, every lovely inch, heightened by the knowledge that she let him. He watched the tops of her breasts quiver under the thin cotton blouse. He'd learned to assess subtle changes in body language and heart rate. He noticed the blush in her cheeks and the red blotches on her chest just below the delicate V of the top of her breastbone. His gaze roamed over her quivering chest again, and he smiled. He couldn't wait to hear her response.

"Depends on what?" she asked.

Her brown eyes mirrored truths he wasn't sure he'd divulge to himself.

"If it's complicated," he said. "I like *un*complicated." He was telling her something he was trying to convince himself he believed.

She took in a sudden brief inhale. Her gaze quickly diverted to the ocean, giving him a full pure look at her upper torso, every curve and valley, until he thought perhaps he could even taste her skin. What Luke saw in profile was a strong, handsome woman with a body made for hard loving, who was unafraid.

Then she turned back and faced him fully. Her body dropped

to her knees in front of him, so quickly he thought perhaps she'd gotten suddenly ill. "I don't do uncomplicated," she whispered. "I like it *complicated* and rich. I like entangled. I like feeling everything and being sorely missed when I'm gone."

She didn't physically touch him, but she had mated with a part of his body that rarely was visited.

His soul.

He walked around the front of his red Mustang, watching her squirm, crossing those impossible legs on his leather front seat. His pants felt tight from things springing to life. Yup. He had the brass band, the pom-poms and the whole fucking cheering section working on him now. It was going to be an effort to take it slow.

As he opened the driver's door and deposited his stiff torso carefully behind the steering wheel, he knew he wasn't in charge. When he looked at her face, she was staring at his lap.

So much for secrets.

Now that she knew he knew that she knew, it was going to be fucking impossible to go anything slower than the speed of a bullet train.

"I'm between places..." he started to say by way of an apology.

"I have a roommate, and she's home tonight," she said as she frowned. "But I'm okay with a motel."

They were magic words. He leaned across the center console and planted a long languid kiss against her hungry lips, just like the girl in his dream. She wore her perfume subtly somewhere behind her ears or between her breasts, because the mild aroma hooked his chest until he found himself with his arms wrapped around her, pressing her into him, feeling those firm perfect breasts.

Her delicate fingers slid down his thigh and traveled over his erection. She squeezed him, and he thought he would explode. He didn't want her to stop, but he'd make a mess right there in the front seat of his Mustang if they didn't get to a motel quick.

He managed to separate himself but held her fingers in his right hand as he turned the ignition with his left. After the car roared to life, his fingers began seriously having their way with her smooth bottom from inside her waistband, working down. His forefinger had just discovered the warm cleft at the top of her derriere.

She inhaled and leaned back onto him. Her voice was ragged as she whispered, "Hurry."

He clumsily shifted into drive, again with his left hand, and drove one-armed, with his dick big and stiff enough to guide the steering wheel by itself. The Pink Slipper Cottage motel came into view just in time. He thought about saying something like, "I wish I could take you some place nicer," but that would draw too much attention to his meager military salary. Maybe she didn't like sailors. Saying something like, "You're probably used to more expensive places," might indicate he thought she slept around a lot.

Fuck. No, it was safest to just say nothing.

She was all over him as he signed the guest register. The college kid with thick, round glasses seemed not to notice, except he kept clearing his throat and swallowing hard. She slid a hand down the front of Luke's pants, which made him do a reverse whistle with his mouth.

"Luggage?" the clerk asked, and then snapped his eyes shut after stealing a look at her. The young boy was in pain and couldn't control his shaking.

"I'll get it later," Luke answered.

Room 428 was tiny, not that it mattered. As soon as the door closed behind him, she was removing his shirt, her hands riding up the ridges in his chest. The feel of her warm flesh against his, her hair brushing gently against the underside of his chin, the way she shimmied herself out of her shorts with the help of both his hands, was driving him wild with anticipation. He couldn't get them both properly naked fast enough.

She stepped back and allowed a full-length view of her nakedness, her shaved pussy, and the lips of her sex, dipping down like his thirsty tongue. Her knees were spread as she let him come to her, as she twirled a bit of her dark hair between the fingers of her right hand. It was his turn to drop to his knees.

He looked up at her as his hands reached out and barely touched her, at first, then as a lazy forefinger circled her nub and slid up and down her moist passage. He loved looking at the fire building in her eyes as he made her wet, made her coat first one finger, then the other one, then a third as she accepted him fully. She leaned back enough so that he had all the room he needed, fingers digging into his shoulders, in case he might want to bring his face to her peach and drink.

Which of course he did. Happy to oblige. He saw the pink flesh of her full, bowed lips part as his tongue darted around the little button that made her jerk, as he sucked the lovely tangy moisture from her like he needed it to survive. As his fingers smoothed over her ass and tested a slight press against her anus, she didn't shy away. His cock got so stiff, he had to adjust himself with his other hand. And he let her see it.

He was coming alive. He'd held death, but now he was holding the promise of an evening of spilled seed, sweat and anything else they could think of. She waited for him to taste his fill, her long hair falling down to touch the tops of her buttocks as she arched back and moaned.

He took his time with her, which he knew was what she wanted. She'd said she liked entangled. Complicated. Well, hell, he'd give her intense, then he'd worry about the entangled later. Right now it was all about keeping himself in check long enough not to explode all over his knees.

Finally, he stood, looking down at her, holding her face between his hands. With his fingers reaching into the mahogany strands behind her ears, he brought her to his mouth, still wet from her arousal. Before they could meet, she closed the distance, pressed against his hunger, and tasted herself on his lips. His tongue found hers and caressed it as she plunged deep.

Slowly she wrapped one leg around his and slid her wet sex against his thigh. Her breathing was ragged as she told him she couldn't press hard enough, couldn't get enough.

He lifted her with both hands seated below her buttcheeks, and slid her over his erection until her opening got snagged on him.

At this, she tensed. Out of nowhere, she produced a foil packet. He didn't want to set her down, but she was determined he wear something, so he obliged her. Let her lead him over to the bed where she pushed him down, climbed on top and slowly ripped the upper edge of the foil packet. It was one of those fancy pink gizmos with ridges.

Holy goats, how am I going to last?

As if she heard him, she smiled. She pulled the hand he had resting under his head on the starched white pillow and made him help her. Used his fingers to lubricate her opening, then lubricate him, and then covered him with the pink latex. In tandem, they massaged his rock-hard cock up and then down slowly.

Two of his fingers were still inside her when his cock entered her, and she took a quick, deep inhale, before settling herself down on him, laying her legs back and to the side for full penetration. God, he was deep.

They began a rhythmic pattern as she rode him, as she raised herself, and then crushed into him, as her muscles contracted around him, and he started to feel a loss of control.

He'd been clutching one buttcheek so hard, he felt welts on her skin as she removed his hand and rolled over on the coverlet onto her stomach. With one knee raised to her chest, he could see fully her little nude opening, the red glistening folds that beckoned to be touched, kissed, pressed to move aside.

He turned on his side and kissed her there from behind, tilted his head and watched his fingers lose themselves deep inside her again.

She closed her eyes then turned to the pillow, arching up her rear.

He came to his knees and with one finger on her anus button, he positioned himself ready to enter from behind. He rooted her opening. His stiff cock had no trouble navigating the violated, slick tissues of her sex. He plunged deep inside her, deliciously burying himself to the hilt.

He was locked in her lush body, loving the smell of her arousal and the sound of her breaths. He felt her soft flesh against his thighs, against his chest as he hovered over her, digging deep and having as much of her as he could. He couldn't stop himself to properly take his time to explore. That would have to come later. Now it was all about having her or he'd die trying. Or explode like an IED.

She turned her face in profile to him as he continued to pump her from behind. Her mouth drew back in a satisfied smirk that made him lean over and kiss her bunched-up lips. Her eyes grew wide as he filled her, needed her more than he would ever be able to say. He kissed her through her moans, claimed her mouth, all of her.

She rose up on her knees, arched her back, pushing her butt into his lower groin, begging him to go deeper still. She threw back her head, butting his shoulder, panting, pulling him inside her with her fingers reaching behind to clutch his buttcheeks. He wanted to ram so far inside her he was blinded to anything else going on in the room.

Her spasms tightened her opening around him. She held her breath, then shuddered, and groaned into her release. And he was right there with her, thrusting and holding firm until he could spew out every drop.

This was the part when he always got uncomfortable. Several heartbeats later, he wanted to say something. Something other than "thanks" or "that was great." But again, it was prudent not to say anything at all. He continued to taste and kiss and rub himself against her, every bit of her he could feel. This had been way too fast. He hoped she wasn't disappointed.

She didn't look like she minded. Besides, he had a plan to make it up to her.

He delicately flipped her onto her back, quickly thrust back inside her, and kissed the salty hollow between her shoulder and neck.

She groaned again. Her skin felt like silk. His tongue easily traced a path down over both her nipples as he suckled them slowly, first the right and then the left. Her fingers sifted through his scalp. She traced the arch of his ears, then pulled his face to hers and begged for a deep, penetrating kiss he was only too glad to provide.

He'd fuck her until the sun rose again, and then fuck her again at dawn, and through breakfast if she would let him.

Fuck breakfast. Fuck lunch. Fuck dinner.

He'd found her. He'd finally found her, that woman from his dreams. He'd watched her walk with that tall gait of confidence only the woman meant for him could have. She was someone he could love and love hard. She could love all the sand and dust and death right off him. She would let him show her how much he needed this connection.

And she wouldn't run away.

He was caught, entangled, willingly dying those thousand little deaths as she kissed him. His real, flesh-and-blood dream woman breathing life into him.

Again.

And he would never let her go.

Well, at least not until tomorrow or the next day.

MOUNTAIN
MAN

Tasmin Flowers

Right from the start I knew it was all my fault. It was my idea to go hiking in the late autumn, and me who persuaded Frankie to come, arguing against her better judgment. It was me who left the map in the trunk of the car, and it was me who couldn't be bothered to dig out my hiking boots. Frankie didn't even have any, walking not being her thing, but I told her trainers would be fine. We'd stick to the paths, I said with an airy wave of my hand.

Here are some of the lessons that I learned:

1) Just because it's sunny in the morning doesn't mean the weather's going to stay that way.

2) Fog can come down really fast on a mountain.

3) Trainers offer no support to ankles.

4) Paths can vanish abruptly.

5) Shorts do not keep you warm.

6) Blundering on when you can't see where you're going can lead to accidents.

* * *

The accident happened about two hours after we had lost the path in the fog. I think the right thing to do would have been to immediately retrace our footsteps until we found it again. But that's not what I suggested at the time, so we carried on walking through the scrubby trees and undergrowth, steadily climbing higher and all the time looking for a path.

Emerging onto the ridge was quite unexpected, and that's probably why Frankie slipped and plunged over the other side. And that side was a lot steeper. She suddenly vanished from sight. Then I heard her shriek, and there were scrabbling noises and the sounds of branches breaking.

It was silent again as I gingerly approached the edge.

"Fuck!" she said, and I nearly lost my balance and followed her down. "Fucking ouch!"

She was about twenty feet below me, where the steep slope shelved slightly, and she was clutching on to a bedraggled bush. One of her legs was twisted in a way that didn't look right, and she continued cursing loudly.

"Hold on, I'm coming down to you," I shouted.

Skidding down the slope on my tail I learned something else: gravel can go up your shorts. And that's not a good place for it.

Frankie couldn't straighten her leg and certainly couldn't get up. I made her lie back against the slope to take some of the pressure off, but it was already swelling up, black and blue. There was no way she was going to walk down the mountain, even with my help. And of course, we still didn't even know which was the way back.

Frankie cried with pain, and I cried with, I suppose, self-pity. I didn't know what to do. We called out for help, but the fog deadened the sound of our voices and, anyway, we hadn't seen

anyone else for hours. Not since we'd lost the path. I felt awful
for Frankie but there was nothing I could do. If she tried to
move her leg even an inch, it was agony.

I tried to go for help, but the slope was too steep and slippery with gravel to climb back up. Below us was a black gulley
that we couldn't see the bottom of. I tried to make a move but a
flurry of pebbles bouncing down into infinity made Frankie grip
my arm tightly. I was glad.

"You can't leave me here," she said. "I'm afraid."

"Afraid of what?" I asked. "No bear or person's gonna come
down here."

But I was happier to stay with her.

The day wore on, and we had no food and no drink. Frankie
was shivering. I was getting desperate. I didn't know what to do,
but I knew it was up to me to do something. That's when my
imagination started playing tricks on me. Voices singing in the
distance. A burst of sunshine through the fog. The herbs-and-
garlic smell of my favorite Italian restaurant. The *whop-whop-
whop-whop* of helicopter blades.

The *whop-whop-whop* of a helicopter! Coming closer and
far too loud to be imaginary.

"Hooray! We're saved," I cried, hugging Frankie, as the fog
was blown away by the dark silhouette of a chopper above us.

She winced in pain, and I gently let her go.

"So where are they going to land?" she asked. "They're probably not even looking for us."

But thankfully she was wrong. Seconds later a man in a
bright-orange Mountain Rescue tunic and helmet was being
winched down to us on the bottom of a rope. And what a man!
He landed on our shelf, unclipped his rope and took my breath
away. Six-foot-four of mountain muscle come to take command
of the situation. My chest heaved with relief.

"Either of you ladies hurt?" he asked, shouting to be heard above the whopping.

I pointed at Frankie's leg and he dropped to his knees beside her. After a cursory look, he swung a pack off his back and removed his helmet.

At which point I was truly lost. No one who's on a rescue mission has a right to be that good looking. Not when saving a person's life already gives him such an advantage. His face could have been sculpted out of granite, with sheer cheekbones, a strong jaw and a long, straight nose. But it was anything but stony. His bright-blue eyes were like sparks of electricity, while the sensuous curve of his red lips sent a jolt of current right through me. And my fingers were straightaway itching to rake through his tousled blond hair.

But his attention was, quite rightly, on Frankie. He tentatively felt her ankle with a large, tanned hand, and she squealed. Moving his hand away quickly, he pulled a radio handset out of his tunic pocket.

"Okay, drop the basket," he said into the radio. "Looks like a broken leg."

He turned to me. "What about you? You okay?"

I nodded. I didn't think cold and scared would really cut it with a guy like this.

"All right, ladies, this is what's happening. You," he said, pointing at Frankie, "are going up in the stretcher and straight to hospital. Which means you," pointing at me, "and I get left here. The chopper can't fit the stretcher and an extra passenger, so it'll be back for us in the morning."

I gulped. "That would be tomorrow morning?" Was I competing for the gold star in stupidity?

Those blue eyes studied me for a moment, and I could have sworn the corners of his mouth were twitching. But he didn't seem to feel the need to answer. *I get it,* I thought. *The strong and silent type.*

Fifteen minutes later and I was waving Frankie good-bye as, strapped into an orange plastic basket that made her resemble an Egyptian mummy, she was winched up into the helicopter.

"Love you, sweetie," I shouted after her, but I don't think she heard me through the noise of the blades.

Then she was scooped in through the door and the chopper swooped away in a giant arc, the noise of the rotors receding with it.

The silence rang in my ears.

"I'm Jake, by the way," said a voice so loud I nearly jumped out of my skin. "Yeah, I know, I can stop shouting now," he added not so loudly.

I grinned through chattering teeth. "Melody."

"Pretty name." Then his face suddenly darkened. "So what the hell were you two girls playing at?"

"We got lost, and then Frankie fell." I felt a little indignant at his tone. "It could have happened to anyone."

"Anyone who didn't have a map or the right shoes or appropriate clothing."

So my knight in shining armor was actually a bit of jerk. I turned away from him. I'd been through enough, and I didn't need to take anymore.

"Hey, Melody, I'm talking to you."

I ignored him.

"My pilot has risked his life flying in fog to help you and your friend. You do realize that, don't you?"

How to make someone feel really good about herself, step one: imply that she might be the cause of another person's possible demise.

"And you were damn lucky it was only fog. It can snow up

here at this time of year. I have a good mind to take you over my knee..."

This was too much and I burst into tears. It was his turn to feel bad.

"Sorry," he mumbled, looking down at the ground. "You're cold."

The stretcher, when it was winched down, had contained a supply pack to see us through the night. Jake unzipped it and pulled out an orange Mountain Rescue fleece.

"Here, put this on."

My coloring dictates that orange isn't really the color for me, but for the first time in my life I positively embraced it. Color me Day-Glo, as long as it's warm.

"So what else you got in there?" I was hungry and thirsty.

The survival pack was pretty well equipped, in fact. There was food and water, with a tiny primus stove to heat them, a medical pack and two huge silver survival blankets. But best of all, a large bar of chocolate, which I attacked as soon as I saw it.

Jake set up the little stove with a practiced air, and we dined on prepacked beef stew with carrots, and I was so hungry that it didn't taste at all bad. Actually fucking delicious, if the truth be known. While we ate, Jake told me about some of the more dramatic rescues he'd been on. This evidently wasn't one of them. Then, after we'd both finished our stew, Jake brewed up some instant coffee.

By this time the fog had thickened to a dense, dark gray and the light was already failing. Jake had to use a torch to pour the joe into a couple of tin cups, and I started to get a feeling like I was a frontierswoman out on the trail.

"Okay, I'm putting out the torch now to preserve the battery," he said.

"So why don't we light a fire to keep warm?" I suggested. No ulterior motive, I promise you.

"Firstly, Melody, you might have noticed that the few pieces of wood there are on this slope are wet from the fog. But also, we're in a national park and that would be breaking the rules."

Geez. What a fun guy.

"I don't suppose that survival pack had any whisky we could add to this," I said gesturing with my cup.

Jake laughed.

"Stuck out on a mountain, and you wanna party. I gotta admire your style, Melody. You're pretty cool."

I basked for a moment, but I couldn't help but wonder how we were going to pass the time.

"It's cold. Come on, let's get these blankets sorted," he said.

He put the torch back on and unfolded the survival blankets. Baco-foil on one side and bright Mountain-Rescue orange on the other side. I couldn't really see how the incredibly thin, light "blankets" were going to keep us warm. But Jake got busy with some tape from the medical kit and had soon fashioned a narrow sleeping bag out of the two.

I watched with interest. One sleeping bag, two people. How was that going to work?

"Shared body heat," said Jake, as if he could read my mind. "My lucky night. I get to share the sleeping bag with you."

"So that's why you joined the Mountain Rescue? So you could share your body heat with young, vulnerable females?"

Jake grinned, and I felt a delicious fluttering deep in my stomach.

"It's usually old men with wind problems," he said.

"Okay. Too much information there."

He took off his boots and wriggled into the sleeping bag. I took off my trainers slowly. I wanted to savor the moment while I could still imagine that something was going to happen between us. He held up the rim of the sleeping bag so I could slide in next to him. I took the plunge.

It was a tight squeeze, and as we were both still fully dressed it mostly felt like being cocooned in fabric. But my face was level with his neck. I breathed in deeply to get the smell of him and—wow! Man-sweat, musk, sandalwood... I had to concentrate hard on not breathing heavily. God, I'd always had dreams about being rescued from peril by a handsome lunk and, boy, was this living up to the fantasy. I wriggled to get comfortable on the hard ground and breathed in deeply again. My hips tried to go on an exploration of their own, but I managed to keep them still.

Jake slid an arm under my shoulders and raised me up a bit against his chest.

"Lean on me," he said. "It'll be more comfortable than the ground."

I could feel the warmth of his body through my Day-Glo layers as I snuggled against him. "So it's true..." I whispered with a sigh.

"What?" he said. His breath tickled my ear, making part of my insides flip.

"That thing about body heat. I feel warm already."

"Hot," he said.

We both turned toward each other at the same moment, so we were lying chest to chest. My breath caught in my throat as I realized we were also hip to hip. His burgeoning response to our shared body heat was pressing against my stomach.

I raised my face. It was too dark to see his expression, but his ragged breathing told me all I needed to know. I slipped a hand to the back of his neck and pulled his head down to mine. Our lips met in a kiss that was anything but gentle, and his tongue pushed its way into my willing mouth immediately. It plundered and took possession, skirting the edges of my teeth, exploring the hollows of my cheeks, caressing my tongue and searching ever deeper until our teeth knocked against each other. Both his hands came up and raked through my hair, pulling my head back to tilt my mouth higher, and the erection I felt pressing against me was now huge and hard.

Inside the sleeping bag was a furnace, our bodies smoldering against each other, breaking out in the sweat of anticipation. There was no stopping what was coming down the track toward us, and I didn't want to.

His mouth pulled back from mine, and his hands ran down my back. They were wide enough to cover the whole width of it. When they reached my waist, I felt his fingers burrowing up under the hem of my fleece.

"It wouldn't do for you to get too hot," he breathed in my ear. "We'd better get this top off you."

"Is this what they teach you in Mountain Rescue school?"

"Science has proven it's the best way to keep warm."

"I see," I said. "And you take your job seriously?"

"It's all part of the service, ma'am."

He pulled the fleece and my T-shirt up over my head in one swift move and tucked them under his head to form a pillow. I was still lying on his chest, and the rough material of his Mountain Rescue tunic grazed my nipples. A fire sprung deep in my loins, and I pushed my hips hard against his.

As his cool hands cupped my breasts, I felt my nipples springing to attention. A whimper escaped me and I caught his bottom lip between my teeth with a nip.

"Your top..." I could barely speak I was so turned on.

"It's coming off." His voice was equally husky. He wanted me as much as I wanted him.

But moving within the tight confines of the survival blankets wasn't easy; it was like dancing a slow horizontal waltz. Jake wriggled his arms down to undo his uniform tunic, while I tried to move to one side to give him room. There was the click of a press stud and then the slow grind of a zip—and never have I heard a sexier sound in my life. I pushed up his T-shirt as he struggled out of it, and explored the new territory offered. His chest was warm and firm with smooth skin, and I could feel the rise of his well-developed pecs. I dropped my mouth down and my tongue sought out a nipple, causing Jake to groan and flex his hips.

"Oh, baby," he moaned.

His hands found their way back to my breasts, and he squeezed and pulled on my nipples, making them burn and setting red-hot currents coursing through my body to its epicenter.

Without thinking, I moved my hands to the top of his pants and slipped them inside. But as I started to slowly explore the top of his shorts, one of my elbows stuck out and tore through the edge where the two blankets were taped together.

"Shit," I said.

But Jake didn't care. He ripped the blankets apart so we could have more room for maneuver. After all, neither of us was cold now. As my hands unfastened his pants and slid them down, he did the same with my shorts. We were both breathing heavily and his musky smell hitting my nostrils played havoc with my hormones. I was wet and ready, and as he pulled my panties down, they left a sticky trail right down to my ankles.

His fingers delved deep into the crevice between my legs, and I arched toward him to open the path. At the same time I felt the fingers of his other hand searching out my clit, and he caught it between finger and thumb, sending a jolt of electricity up through me, making me gasp.

"Have you got a condom?" I could hardly form the words.

He nodded, biting my earlobe and sending a tremor down my spine.

"Essential part of the survival kit."

"Don't make me wait," I begged.

A few seconds of rifling through his tunic pockets, a rip of foil and then I was helping him roll the latex down his cock. And, god, what a cock! Soft as velvet on the outside, rock solid within. I could hardly encircle it with my hand. Getting this inside me was going to be a stretch, but I had to have it.

"You're so wet," he said, as he rolled me onto my back and pushed my legs apart.

Then I felt the nudge of his magnificent cock against the side of my pussy. As I raised my hips to meet him, he took the plunge. It was tight and it hurt, but in a good way, the best way. I yelped with delight. He didn't go in too deep and slowly withdrew. Then he plunged again, farther now, as I stretched to accommodate him. And then again, driving deeper each time and harder. Grunting with exertion, he pounded me into the rough stony ground. Each thrust sent a surge of white-hot, molten sensation ripping through me. His mouth dropped down to my right breast, his tongue teasing the nipple, adding another layer of intensity. I wrapped my legs around his waist and raked my hands through his damp hair. One of his hands crept down between my legs, and then two fingers slowly circled my clit. He'd brought me to the brink, and I knew that in a split second I'd be tumbling, out of control, carried by the torrent of pleasure he was unleashing deep within me.

With a roar and a moan, we climaxed together, our bodies arching against each other as the head of his cock nudged against my cervix, the muscles of my pussy convulsing around him to squeeze out every last drop. A final thrust and my orgasm undid me. I fell back with my arms above my head as my hips thrust harder against him, and then slowly relaxed to release him from my grasp. Our chests were slick with sweat, and when he slumped down on top of me, our lips met in a languorous kiss.

"I think I feel properly rescued now," I whispered in his ear.

"You should survive the night," he replied, pulling the blankets around us and enveloping me in his arms.

You may not believe it, but I had the best night's sleep ever, half-naked on the side of mountain with a man I barely knew. But it's true. I awoke, snuggled against his chest, to hear the *whop-whop-whop* of the returning chopper.

Jake sat bolt upright leaving me sprawling on the ground beside him.

"Quick, get dressed," he said.

Minutes later, we were in the belly of the bird, being flown back to civilization. Jake gave me a pair of headphones to put on to cut out the noise of the rotors and allow us to talk to each other.

"Morning, Jake," said the pilot's voice in my ear. "Glad to have you back on board."

"Morning, Sam," said Jake, grinning at me as our eyes met.

"Just one thing," said Sam. "I was wondering, but I couldn't work it out; why did you tell me not to come back for you last night?"

"Yes, why was that, Jake?" I asked, smiling widely.

Funny thing, but Jake didn't have an answer.

THE STAR

Tahira Iqbal

I've picked the wrong day to come to the cemetery. It is raining so hard my hair is wet within moments after the wind catches my umbrella and turns it inside out.

I miss a puddle, but not the next one, the water sloshing over my heels and dampening my toes as I quickly make my way over the sodden turf while fixing my umbrella. I didn't have time to change out of my office clothes after leaving work early. I'd been keen to get out of London before the rush-hour traffic. But being chilled by the cold, the rain...it doesn't matter. Nothing does anymore. He's here, and I want to see him.

Carefully finding my way through the graves, I stoop down to pat the headstone, feeling how smooth it is, so very brand new, not aged like some of the markers deeper in the cemetery. The gold scroll of the words my parents and I had chosen is eloquent and heartfelt; the letters gleam against the sparkling black granite, the rainwater caught in the etching.

"Hello, Dean."

I remove my cold hand to jam it into a pocket, and tears rise freely as I step back, looking at the patch of earth that now keeps my brother. I live over a hundred miles away; my parents had of course wanted Dean to be buried close to their village, so I am only able to visit him when I come to see them.

Six months. Six long, aching months since we'd received notification that their brave son, my brave brother in the Royal Air Force, had been killed in action. We'd tried to shelter my mother from the extent of his fatal injuries, but she had wanted to know everything, especially questioning why we couldn't have an open casket.

Nightmares had given me twisted visuals of what had become of him. Awful hours where horrors occurred and showed me a sibling I didn't recognize. I'd pleaded to the heavens, on my knees on hot desert sand, for him to be...restored.

Days would go by, and all I could think of was him: tall, broad, funny and serious at the same time. The coolest older brother, the utterly skilled pilot who delivered effective force where it was needed but never without great thought and planning for the innocents on the ground. I'd lost my brother, my best friend, but I was proud of him, and his decision to defend. That didn't curb the ache inside, something I knew would stay with me forever.

I shiver now as the wind blows, creeping under the battered umbrella and the collar of my coat. Sunset is breaking the horizon apart. "I better go Dean, I'll see you soon." I lay the small bunch of flowers against the fresh bundle that my mother had left earlier in the week before heading to the car.

That's when I see him. The stranger standing beside my car. My heart picks up speed as he begins to walk toward me. He's dressed in dark clothes, perhaps denims and a jumper with an unzipped parka that's now wet from the rain, like his hair.

The tall, handsome, blue-eyed man stops a few yards from me.

He looks past me, to the spot I've just stood on, then back at me, those intense eyes, lit like the brightest sky, sending a rare shot of warmth to cradle the hope that's almost dead inside of me.

"I'm Calder."

I nod with understanding. The man who had only appeared as short sharp descriptions in even shorter emails, had become like family to Dean. He had said that Calder was the best comrade from another country's army anyone could have.

"I'm sorry for your loss." His American accent is a rich vibration of power.

I nod again, my voice hidden in the depths of my surprise.

"I got home from my tour last week. Bought a ticket and here I am."

I try for a smile. "I'm Estella."

"I know who you are, ma'am."

My eyes fill with tears; I brush them away quickly. "Um, I'm sure my parents would like to meet you. Do you have time to visit them?"

"Your mom and dad are on my list," Calder says. "So are you."

And that's when I lose it. "I really wish I wasn't..." I whisper, "then Dean would still be here."

Calder looks at the grave again, his shoulders squaring. "Even if he was...I know that I'd want to meet you, the way your brother talked about you, the way he cared for you even though he was thousands of miles away."

The offer to drive him to my parents' home is declined for the moment. Instead, I take him to his hotel in the center of the village.

"I'll be in touch," Calder says before leaving the car with my phone number.

I don't sleep well that night. I've been given my old room, and even though it has been cleared of all my childhood paraphernalia there are moments when I expect Dean to pop his head around the door frame, tease me about my latest experimental hairstyle or ask me a question (or ask me to do the sums) for his math homework.

Rising early, I find the house dim, quiet and warm. I stop at Dean's room. He had his own place, a small apartment in a nearby town, but he'd left lots of his personal items here before shipping out.

I reach for a photo frame. Dean in his pristinely pressed uniform, smiling, giving me a comforting hug as we'd said good-bye for his first deployment. That had been nearly eight years ago.

He'd come home a different man after his first tour of duty. Quieter, but with an intensity that had created a force field around him I couldn't quite break through. We might not have been kids anymore, but still we joked around, reverting to our silly teenage selves when we were with each other. But he'd been *gone* in certain respects; in his place was a razor-sharp *soldier*.

My cell trills in my room, so I head back. It's Calder, checking whether tomorrow morning would be okay to visit my parents. I reply quickly, confirming the visit as I've already spoken to them the previous evening, and then curl up in bed thinking of the American.

Lieutenant Peter Calder, United States Air Force, Dean had written once, *the man can cut paper just by looking at it.*

It's after eleven A.M. when I finally wake the following day, and I can hear Calder's striking voice drifting upstairs. "Damn it." I'm edgy and clammy as I'd been taken in by a nightmare that had held on so tight I'd been unable to fight it. I'd walked through a battlefield filled with bodies to where normally Dean would have stood.

But now it was Calder who was there, his hand open and waiting. Behind him in the distance, his F-16 billowed smoke from where its tail should have been. I extended my hand but everything had disappeared into a booming cloud of pure white light and heat as something long and pointed arrived with a screech to crash and explode between our feet, throwing us apart. In pieces.

Washing quickly, I change and head downstairs. Calder rises out of his seat with a welcoming smile. "Good morning, Estella." The good manners make me blush a little as I enter the room.

My terrible night's sleep is forgotten.

The group is sitting with teacups and an assortment of baked goods my mother can't quite stop making. Something about idle hands comes to mind and the ache returns again.

I try not to smile as Calder's big fingers attempt to lift the delicate china cup. I heat inwardly as I imagine those fingers exploring *other* places.

My parents talk with Calder quietly as I go to refill the teapot. In the act of searching for a mug for him, I *feel* him walk into the room.

Furtively he says, eyes sparkling, "I'm looking for something larger than this thimble to drink the tea out of... Ah, great minds..."

I hold up the mug, offering it. Calder takes it, our fingers brushing. I'm electrified by the crush in my heart.

He smiles, and I know he doesn't do it often because his handsome face is free of laughter lines. Something inside sharpens, and I have to blink back the despair, "Do you want to go for a walk?"

Wrapping up warm against the chilly morning, Calder and I set off on foot for the village, beside us nothing but fields covered in waist-high mist.

"Dean said you met at a U.K. versus U.S. football match on the base?"

"Yeah, he was the goalie, and I kicked him when I should have kicked the ball."

"Ouch." I laugh, comforted by Calder's magnetic presence. I can see why Dean got on with him, although what I'm feeling is *totally* different.

"You should know that Americans aren't really good at soccer. Give me any other sport, and I'll kick your ass."

"Yeah, he said they won, what, eight goals to one?" I say with a smile, checking the winding lane before crossing over to the path. I unhook the gate, letting Calder pass through before securing it again. "Now, *that* had to hurt."

"Yeah, it kinda dented the unit's pride, but we became friends after that."

"Friendship was the least you could offer. I mean, you did kick him in the jewels."

Calder laughs so deeply a cow grazing in the next field looks up at us.

The silence extends as we walk side by side, close enough I can feel his jacket brush mine.

"Were you there?"

"When it happened? No, I was flying in another part of the country with my own unit."

I exhale deeply, eyes blurring, and come to a halt.

"Hey..." Calder's hand goes to my shoulder as he faces me.

"If you say something like, it was quick and painless..." I draw myself away.

"I'm not going to say that..." he says darkly as we both know the awful truth. The casket had been sealed for a reason.

"Good, bullshit doesn't help." Tears sting the backs of my eyes as I try to walk away.

"Stop." Calder turns me around, putting both his palms against my face. "You're not sleeping are you?"

I lower my eyes

"Nightmares?"

"Calder..."

"You can tell me."

"No," I say shakily, "what you guys face is worse than whatever I'm going through."

"Estella," he says quietly, his thumbs brushing my cheekbones, the tears. "War zones are wherever you make them."

We arrive at the village pub, and once I've introduced Calder to the landlord, I'm touched by the offer of free drinks: a coffee for Calder and a tea for me. We drink in silence. I'm affected by what he said in the field so I focus on the roaring and crackling fire we're sitting beside.

"We better head back to your mom and dad's," Calder says reaching for his jacket once we're done, his head nearly scraping the beams of the ancient building.

"That's okay. Your hotel is right around the corner, I'd just be driving you back anyway..."

"I'm walking you home, Estella." He reaches for my coat, and helps me into it, "Let's go."

Once we're outside, he puts his hand into mine.

The hope inside...*ignites.*

We approach the house. "Why don't you stay at my place?" The suggestion seems to throw him as he looks down at me with something in his eyes I can't quite read. "Er... I mean...you've never been to London right? Why don't you take some nice memories back home at least?"

"I'd like that."

"I mean...you'll be sleeping on the couch...maybe a hotel would be better?"

"Estella," his fingers lightly squeeze mine, "the couch is fine."

Three hours later, Calder and I arrive at my flat on the outskirts of London.

"So what do you want to do first?" I flip through my phone checking out some of the tourist information apps I'd downloaded when we'd returned to my parents house.

"This."

He's got me in his arms suddenly, his lips to mine. The hunger, the urgency steals my breath and puts a tingle in the backs of my knees.

"I wanted to do that all morning." His palm, big and broad, presses into my back, rubbing softly. "Come with me."

We find ourselves at my bedroom door.

Color heats my face, which Calder notices.

"Relax... I just want you to rest, sleep, okay?" He brushes the hair off my shoulders with such care I break down, bawling my eyes out. Calder holds me until I've composed myself enough to climb onto the bed with him. He takes me into his arms so that I can rest against his chest.

I don't know how long I stare down at the length of his denim-clad legs, but when my eyes droop shut, I don't fight it.

The nightmare attacks with its usual bite. This time I've made it through the body-strewn war zone, my hand reaching for Calder, the tension in my chest reaching the boiling point as I anticipate the arrival of the missile.

His fingers curve around mine, and the white light doesn't come. He brings me up against the warmth of his body, his uniform rough against my clothes, a gun at his side, poised and ready to take down anything that will hurt me...or us.

"Hey." Softness in the dark, a cool voice brings me home. I open my eyes. Calder. "You were dreaming?"

I swallow back the worry. "It was different this time."

"How?" Calder traces a finger along my lips.

"You got to me in time."

A victorious smile makes his lips part as he leans in for a kiss. Calder sighs against my mouth, his erection hard against my thigh.

"Estella..." he groans, "are you sure you don't want me on the couch?"

I smile against his lips, laughing softly, "Maybe later."

The soldier looks at me, eyes hot. "Done."

My laughter ceases when his hand travels to my zipper. With an achingly languid and erotic pace, he slides it down before slipping his hand inside my panties to cup me.

I screw my eyes tight shut, vaulting into something sparkling and definite.

Slowly, with one fingertip, he rubs, drawing a cascading wetness within that heralds a complete shift of my senses.

He kisses my throat reverently. I uncurl my fists and reach between us, panting as I reach for the buttons of his shirt. He's hard. All over. I run my hands over his torso, fingers falling into the dents and design of his muscles, especially the ridges of his abs. His groan of pleasure is a sound I know I'm going to be addicted to.

I push the shirt off his shoulders, before working his belt, followed by his button fly.

I push the material, but can't get past midthigh.

"Here..." He sits up, swiveling his feet to the floor before standing. Quickly, he drags his denims and boxers off, revealing his erection.

Absorbed by his visually arresting arousal, I quickly haul my shirt off; I reach around for my bra.

"No..." He kneels beside me. "Let me."

Without breaking eye contact, he reaches for the clasp at the back, snaps it apart and slowly brings it down my arms. His inhale is broken once he lets his gaze travel down to my breasts. I sink back against the linens and he kisses each nipple before reaching down and tugging my panties off.

I trace the muscle of his shoulder with my lips, awed by his build. I close my eyes as he places soft, light kisses against my neck which make me part my legs. I feel his searching cock, which he guides into me. I watch fascinated as inch by inch he disappears inside of me.

His thrusts are slow, steady, creating a heat within that threatens to obliterate anything in its path. Including my grief. Tears push into my eyes and fall.

"Estella? What's wrong? Jesus! Am I hurting you?"

I shake my head. "Just don't stop... Calder, don't stop." I am astounded by the fit of him and the power of this sudden union.

Calder kisses my temple, reverently whispering my name. And that does it. My tears explode and something within breaks free. I drag his head down, opening his mouth with mine, pushing my tongue inside.

Calder's thrusts get stronger, faster, deeper as the fury of emotion makes us both breathless.

I come first, grabbing his buttocks for support as I shake with a momentous curl of passion that finally shuts out the darkness I've been walking in.

"I'm close," Calder whispers against my mouth.

My heartbeat breaks through into new territory, and I encourage his climax by squeezing my muscles around him, which makes him groan. I clutch at him, marveling at how hard he is, making sure he's gaining what he needs from this moment.

"Estella..." With one final, hard push, Calder comes inside of me. He collapses against my breast and this time, I welcome the weight.

Later, I watch him dozing beside me, sprawled out on his back. I pull the comforter, tugging it over our naked bodies. Calder wakes and reaches for me. I fit my back against his chest; his arms loop around me.

Delicate, soft kisses meet the back of my neck. I push my buttocks into him, feeling him stir.

"More?" he says sleepily.

I laugh.

"Couch?" he asks.

I toss back the covers and run, Calder following. Catching up with me, he puts his warm hands on my hips, which unleashes a squeal of delight as we stumble nude into the living room.

He guides me to the couch, and I kneel on it, facing the wall, bracing my hands against it. He drops barely there kisses along the length of my spine. "I like hearing you laugh," he says, as he gently pulls my legs apart.

I gasp shakily. "I like that sound too."

Settling behind me, he then reaches around my hip. Calder slides a finger, then another along my wetness. My head tips back, resting just below his shoulder as he winds his other hand around my waist, his hard cock pointing north as it presses against the base of my spine. He works slowly, achingly slowly, until he's knuckle deep inside of me. Withdrawing, he then rests the pads of his fingers on my clit, circling it.

I'm soaked and on the way to being sated in a way I've never felt before. I can't help but moan his name as I come, trembling breathlessly from the vibrancy of the orgasm.

I twist my head, reach for his mouth with my own before Calder withdraws and makes me sit astride his hips and pushes up inside of me.

"How will you watch over me when you're so far away?" I whisper, placing my hands into his, our fingers looping, enhancing our connection.

"Your name, it means 'star', right?" he whispers back, his voice rough with passion as he looks up at me.

"Right," I sigh, getting wonderfully hot all over again as I undulate over him.

"Then I'll be with you in the sky every time I fly," he says, eyes luminous with duty.

I close my eyes and breathe, letting the light fully break free within.

PITCH BLACK

Delilah Devlin

Given the right company and a soft bed, Danny Crispin would have welcomed the hot summer storm. He'd have opened his bedroom curtains, tossed up the window and let the wet wind howl right inside. Wouldn't matter if his bed got saturated. The thought of a certain redhead covered in rain and sweat, green eyes glinting hotter than any flash of lightning, tightened his body.

However, a thunderstorm spelled trouble this night. He gazed up from behind the wheel of the prison pickup and watched yet another brilliant flash dance and pop across the strands of the concertina wire high atop the chain-link fence.

"Sarge, did you see that?" the radio squawked, all formal radio protocols forgotten by the new guard in the South Tower.

Danny understood Officer First Class Hughes's concern. The towers were open metal cages, no glass in the windows to protect the guards from the elements. No doubt the young officer had parked his weapon in a corner, his metal chair beside it, and stood in his rain poncho with his rubber-soled boots on the iron grating while rain sliced sideways, soaking him. It's what he'd done when he'd been a rookie corrections officer, before he'd been promoted to sergeant a year ago.

Another jagged bolt sparked on the wire, and he cursed, wishing he was back in his hub keeping watch on the restless prisoners. Jenna Hurly was scheduled to be in the barracks. If the power went out, she'd be trapped in the dark with eighty murderers. He hoped like hell the storm blew over soon, and he could head back to the Hub One cell block. Half an hour ago, the lieutenant had ordered him to assume his rover duties outside the fence so he could be inside the walls in case the power went out and generators had to be cranked to replace the feed from the electric company. Something that occurred with annoying frequency in this remote region of Arkansas.

Danny drove a slow circle around the dirt track surrounding the walls. The rain fell harder, the wiper blades useless against the deluge, his headlights barely piercing the darkness.

Moments later, another flash was followed by a loud explosion. Then the lights in the two towers in his line of sight went dark, confirming his worst fears. The transformer had been hit.

Danny pressed the gas and clicked the button on his radio. "Grayson, meet me at the North Tower!"

Moments later, he skidded to a halt in the mud. Because the automatic locks wouldn't be working, he had his keys in hand, his flashlight held at his shoulder as he ran toward the gate. He opened it just as Grayson came running. "You take rover. I'm going inside."

Corporal Grayson gave him a curt nod as they passed each other. Danny turned to lock the gate behind him then ran toward the entrance of the prison, the pitch darkness inside the glass doors ominous. Again he fought the lock then raced through the corridor toward his hub.

He ran to the North Control booth. They couldn't pop the button, so again he was delayed opening the locks to first the outer door, then the inner door. Not slowing, he ran right, passing Central Control, then hit a quarter turn to the left and arrived at the Plexiglas corridor that usually gave a bird's-eye view into Hubs One and Three.

Eerie darkness spread beneath him. At the end of the corridor he entered another door and another, then passed Hub One's control booth where he spared a second to wave at Officer McGee, whose concern was etched in his wrinkled face.

As Danny raced through a rabbit's warren of doors and stairs, his heart thudded dully against his chest. He hoped like hell Jenna had kept her head, followed their preset plan, and that she'd be waiting in the tiled shower area of the barracks. With the power out, the prisoners would be making the most of the unsupervised time. Images of vicious beatings and rapes flashed through his mind. A male officer faced horrific dangers, but a female caught on the floor...

He couldn't think about that now and not go nuts. He had to keep calm. Had to get to her. As he at last entered the third tier of the barracks, he flicked off his flashlight and felt for the iron bars atop the stairs and followed them, jostling past prisoners moving in the darkness.

Two more flights down, she'd be there. Waiting in the darkness. If he was lucky the skinheads had gotten to her first. They'd stepped in a couple of times to prevent assaults, having decided Officer Hurly was "good people."

Relying on a lifer wasn't Danny's idea of the optimal situation, but an officer caught in the midst of a melee didn't have many choices. Hiding in the darkness, her back against a wall, hoping no one heard her breathe or noted where she was when the lights went out...

Danny drew a deep breath to calm his heart and barreled down the last of the iron stairs.

The moment the lights flickered out, Jenna darted to the left, through the last "hole" between prisoners where she'd been patrolling, keeping an eye on the restless bunch.

Her radio squawked. "Grayson, meet me at the North Tower!"

Thank god. Danny was on his way. She reached for her radio and turned it off. The sound would pinpoint her location to those around her. Then she slipped her cuffs from her back pocket, slid one manacle around her wrist and gripped the other like brass knuckles. Just in case she had to fight her way through.

Already she heard hard thuds, no doubt the sound of battery packs wrapped in socks hitting flesh. Soon after, the slick sounds of an illicit tryst came from beside her, but she stilled her breaths, held out her hands and moved as quickly as she could, her metal cuff and pepper-spray can held at the ready in case she found trouble.

"Red," a husky whisper sounded beside her, using the nickname the prisoners had given her, but never dared say to her face. She was Officer Hurly to them all.

But she recognized the voice of the whisperer. For a second, she felt relief, but then she remembered the crime Prisoner Draper had committed. Murder. Of three gang rivals. With his bare hands.

She remained silent and still.

"Red," he said a little louder. "Gotta trust me on this, ma'am."

And because she was already turned around in the dark, afraid she hadn't moved fast enough or that someone else would find her, she answered. "Draper, I'm here."

In the inky dark she felt a hand clamp around her wrist. She shook her arm.

"It's me." The whisper came beside her ear. "Coats and Benny are with me. Where you headed?"

She drew a deep breath. If she told them, and they were using her for bait, Danny would be in danger too.

"Where to?" came the gruff whisper. "This lasts too long we'll all be in a world of hurt."

"Showers," she whispered back, biting her lip and hoping she wasn't making the worst mistake of her life.

He pulled on her arm, urging her forward, swiftly, jumbling past bodies beginning to bunch around them. More sickening thuds followed them, but Draper wasn't deterred. In seconds, the sounds around them were more hollow. She reached out a hand and felt cool tile.

"Stand here. We'll keep you safe."

It was a crazy upside-down world. A guard needing to be guarded. There in the dark. Vulnerable in a way she'd prepared for, but never really experienced. Day-to-day working in a prison was fraught with dangers, but this was something darker. Something monstrous.

But for the moment, she felt relief. She firmed her grip on her pepper spray and cuff, spread her feet, prepared to fight and listened for sounds that might indicate others had found them.

After what seemed an hour but could only have been minutes, she heard more shuffling steps entering the shower. Strained whispers. A hand reached out and touched her shoulder, her hair.

She tensed, ready to swing.

"Jenn, it's me."

She sprang forward into Danny Crispin's strong arms.

"I'll take lead," said Draper, his tone harder. He'd never hidden his hatred of the male officers. Likely wished he could have a go at Danny. "You follow," he rasped. "Coats and Benny, take the rear."

Danny shoved her behind him. "Hold onto my shirt. Whatever happens, don't let go."

They made their way slowly out of the shower. Lights flickered around them. Prisoners not using their battery packs as weapons had begun to fashion makeshift flashlights. They were on the hunt. For her, she knew it deep in her bones.

Keeping to the side of the wall, her band of protectors moved out of the showers, toward the first tier's steps. Then they climbed, the sounds of Draper cursing and threatening filling the air as he pushed through the men milling on the steps. Once on the first deck, they rushed toward the stairs at the far end, running now because hollow stomps trailed behind them.

Jenna concentrated on holding onto Danny's shirt, afraid she'd trip and they'd be trapped or pushed through the wide bars to the concrete floor below.

Sharp slaps and thuds surrounded them. Fights and sex. She could picture it, but still couldn't see. She kept silent until a beam of light flashed in her eyes, and the whispers surrounding her grew to satisfied laughter and shouts.

Then the eerie catcalls began. "Hey, Red! Where are you sexy?" Followed by smacking sounds, like wet air kisses.

She shivered in revulsion.

They were nearer now. But her strange band of protectors were on the third tier now, heading toward the fire-safe stairwell. Almost there.

Something slammed into Danny, and he jolted sideways.

Her grip on his shirt loosened. A hand wrapped around her hair and pulled her away. She kicked and slugged at the man holding her. Then there was darkness again, more shoves, and the fingers wound into her hair tugged free. She got to her knees and crawled forward, toward the door.

Behind her, something solid bounced against her buttocks. A hand grabbed for her belt, lifting her to her feet. She swung around, but a beefy arm encircled her waist.

"It's me," Danny said loudly, because now the sounds of an all-out brawl filled the upper deck.

A flashlight shone. The door was just in reach. Danny thrust in the key, turned the lock, and they darted through the door, leaving the battle raging among prisoners behind them.

Danny locked the door then tossed down the flashlight and reached for Jenna. He slid to his ass on the floor, there in the stairwell, his back against the cell-block door. His hands roamed her body, seeking injuries. But he found none. She shivered inside his embrace.

"See why I don't want you here?" he rasped.

"Goes both ways," she whispered harshly, her breaths slowing as she wrapped herself around him. She straddled his hips, bracketed his face between her hands and kissed him hard. "I'm okay. We're both okay. Draper and his buddies had my back."

Danny cussed. "It just as easily could have gone another way. You'd have been at their mercy."

Her feminine huff blew against the side of his neck. "I'm not a hug-a-thug. I know how bad it could have been, but I had to put my trust in someone."

His arms tightened. "I should have been there."

"You had a job, just like me. We've trained for this kind of event. It all worked out."

Anger spiked inside him, heating his face. "Fuckin' hell, Jenn. Fuck the job." Why was she so damn stubborn? There were other jobs in the prison system for chrissakes. He shook his head, biting his tongue to keep from railing at her. This was an old argument, one they had a couple of times a week. If being trapped in the dark with homicidal maniacs wasn't enough to convince her she had no business working inside the prison, he didn't know what would. His shoulders slumped. "I've never been so scared," he whispered, tightening his arms around her.

Again, she snorted. "Scarier than two tours in Iraq?"

Scarier than any firefight he'd lived through when he'd been in the Marines. "Hell, yeah."

Her lips stretched against his cheek.

"Think it's funny?" he growled.

"No, I like that you were so worried." She snuggled closer to his chest. "And I'm relieved as hell you got to me. But won't the LT have your ass for leaving your post?"

"I put Grayson on rover. LT will just have to understand. A female on the floor is every male guard's worst fear."

She sighed. "Shouldn't be that way. I'm just another officer."

So she always said. And he'd never agree. A distant hum sounded. Lights flickered then brightened. Danny blinked against the harsh fluorescence filling the stairwell. "SRT will be suiting up."

She nodded, sighing as she crawled off his lap. "Better go. You'll be busy getting the prisoners back into their cells."

"When shift's over..."

She gave him a nod. "My place."

Danny gave her a lopsided smile. "Don't even think about entering the barracks again."

She tilted her chin. "I'm not crazy."

Reluctant to leave her, he turned her toward the corridor and the hub's control booth. "Stick with McGee."

He gave her ass a slap, and she aimed a glare over her shoulder, then walked with a sway that drew his gaze straight to her round, muscular bottom. Their conversation was far from over. Only talking wasn't going to cut it. Maybe she needed a little dose of reality.

Even through the rattle of the spray hitting her glass shower door, Jenna heard the front door slam. Rinsing the last of the suds from her hair, she turned off the water and tugged her towel from over the edge of the door, wrapping it quickly around her body. By the sound of the heavy thuds of his boots, he was a man on a mission. She had no doubts what was on his mind.

What had been on everyone's mind during the debrief at shift's end. She'd felt the glances, saw the condemnation simmering in the male officers' eyes. Despite the fact females had been serving inside the prison for years, she was a problem. Too pretty. Too slim. A distraction for the prisoners and officers alike.

Things she'd faced down before. No matter how she'd tried to minimize her attraction—no makeup, loose uniforms, her hair pulled into an unflattering, tight bun—she still stuck out like a sore thumb. Danny had to come to her rescue, and that put him in unnecessary danger because guards caught in the dark were supposed to hit a wall and wait. He'd traversed the entire barracks to get her out. Yet no one pointed a finger at him for breaking protocol. They all understood the need.

More than once the LT and the major had offered her easier duty, inside the infirmary or permanently manning a hub's control, but she'd refused, wanting to prove herself. Not because her sole ambition was to be the best corrections office she could be, but because a successful stint there would make her application to the police academy stand out among the other candidates.

Danny knew this. But he didn't support her. Even before they'd begun to see each other, he'd been after her to quit or transfer. When she'd been assigned to his shift, under his command, he'd kept silent about their relationship because he'd been hell-bent on protecting her. Maybe it was time she asked for a transfer to another shift.

The thought left her cold. Because even though things had gone sideways tonight, she'd known he would get to her. No matter what. And that thought had kept her from panic. Not something she would ever let him know.

Her bathroom door slammed open. Still dressed in his uniform, his shoulders spanned the door frame. His short black hair skimmed the upper edge. His dark blue shirt, spattered with raindrops, reflected the stormy color of his eyes as he raked her with a glance. Anger simmered in the glance he gave her.

Her chin shot up. "No, hello darlin'?"

His hand shot out, grabbed her arm and yanked her against his chest. "Fight me."

Her eyes widened. "What's this about?"

He gave a sharp shake of his head. "Shut up. Fight me."

She inserted her free hand between them and shoved at his chest. "Danny?"

"Think you could have fought Draper off if he'd been after you?" he said, his voice a deep, graveled growl.

She swallowed hard against a burning lump at the back of her throat. So that was what this was going to be. A lesson. Proof she wasn't strong enough, mean enough to be on that barracks floor. "Stop this, right now." She pushed again, but he ducked down, shoved his shoulder against her abdomen, forcing her to crumple over him.

Then he was backing out the door, striding toward her bed. He shrugged his shoulder, and she tumbled to the mattress, her towel flying open.

Before she could roll over the side to escape, he was on her, his superior weight sinking her deep into the mattress. Covered shoulder to toe by his large body, she could barely breathe. "Danny."

He shook his head again, a grim set to his tight square jaw. "This ends, Jenn. Tomorrow, you're gonna accept that transfer. Work in the warden's office, guard the nurse, whatever, but you won't be on that goddamn floor."

"You have no right to dictate to me."

"Don't I? Wasn't my ass on the line tonight?"

"I didn't ask—"

"You didn't have to! Dammit, I love you!"

His shout reverberated in the room and had her jaw clamping shut. Bitter tears filled her eyes.

His eyes squeezed shut. Then before she could draw the next shattered breath, he rolled off her to sit at the edge of the bed, his back to her. His shoulders were slumped. "I can't do this again."

The softly spoken words cut through her more sharply than his shouts. Jenna sat up then crawled behind him. He jerked at the first tentative touch of her hand to his shoulder, but she moved closer, wrapping her other arm around his waist and leaning against him. "I'll take the transfer to the infirmary," she whispered.

"I don't want the job to come between us."

"Neither do I. And since this isn't my life's goal, I'll bend. I love you, too."

A deep breath shuddered out. His hands cupped hers against his chest. "I went a little crazy, getting to you."

"I knew you'd be there. Even though I knew you shouldn't come."

His chest billowed around another deep breath, and she relaxed, knowing they'd get past this. That his fear had been real. That he would have faced down eighty men to save her or die trying.

That thought alone made her shiver. "I won't have you watching my back when I'm a cop."

"I'll learn to deal, Jenn. At least, you won't be up against the worst every goddamn day."

She nuzzled her cheek against his shoulder. "Maybe I'm not what you need."

His head swung toward her. His dark-navy gaze caught hers and held. "You're *everything* I need."

The raw texture of his voice made her melt.

He turned and she slid over his spread thighs, straddling him again. His mouth found hers, rubbed once then opened.

She was ready, thrusting her tongue to greet his, suctioning gently to pull his into her mouth. They fed on each other's lips, rubbing, sucking, licking, with more desperate force than finesse. When she leaned back, she glanced down at his chest. "Time to lose that uniform. You smell like pepper spray," she drawled, wrinkling her nose.

"I should shower."

She shook her head. "I don't want to wait. I need you inside me."

With his jaw clamping tight, Danny stood with her in his arms then dumped her on the mattress again. She smiled and set her head on a bent arm to watch as he quickly stripped.

When he was nude, all six-foot-three of ripped muscle and

tanned skin, she went to her knees and peeled back the coverlet, tossed away the pillows, and lay in the center of the bed.

He came at her from the end of the mattress, crawling on his hands and knees, a look of feral concentration on his face, something that set her nerves jangling. God, she loved his fierceness, even when he was angry with her. Maybe especially when he was looking this mean.

Danny Crispin was a primal male, tempered by combat, forged in tragic loss. That he loved her, thought her worthy of all that strength and dedication humbled her. She knew what he needed from her and spread her legs, giving him unspoken submission.

His head dipped between his shoulders, and he buried his face between her legs, breathing in her clean scent, shaking his head side to side as he rubbed his bristled cheeks and jaw between her folds.

The rasp of his beard chafed her delicate skin, but she bent her knees and raised her hips, offering more.

His large hands slipped beneath her, cupped her buttocks. A deep growling moan filled the room a moment before his open mouth sucked her labia inside where his tongue stroked, teasing the shaved lips, delving between to lap up the fluid oozing from inside her.

Jenna kept her hands folded beside her head. Held her body still as he licked up her folds to tease her clit, then back down, beneath her pussy. Her breath caught on a sharp gasp when he flicked the tip of his tongue against her small furled hole.

His gaze darted up; his mouth lifted to give her a wicked, tight smile.

She knew how she looked. Face flushed, her belly beginning to quiver and jump. Her eyes would be large and round, her lips swollen because she'd bitten them and hadn't even known.

Swiping her tongue across her bottom lip, she watched his eyelids dip, his nostrils flare. He dropped her bottom and lunged forward, slipping a hand beneath her back to cradle her close, laying the other atop her breast to squeeze. His head descended, and his mouth took hers in a hard, grinding kiss.

Not that she minded one bit. She tasted herself on his lips. She thrust her hands into his hair, raked his scalp with her nails and bit his tongue, a goad he wouldn't ignore.

Danny gave another growl. His cock slid between her vaginal lips, rocking forward and back, wetting his shaft. She wriggled beneath him, trying to dip lower to capture the tip, but he moved back, so quickly she'd barely blinked her eyes open before he flipped her to her belly.

So he was still in fight mode. She scrambled to get her knees beneath her, faking an attempt to escape, but his hard hands gripped her buttocks, centered her, and his cock nudged once before plunging inside her pussy.

Jenna gave a muffled shout.

He chuckled. The sound was deep and dirty. With his hands, he forced her hips backward, fully sheathing his cock. But then he held still inside her for several long moments.

Jenna got her elbows beneath her and shot a glare over her shoulder. "Gonna move sometime?"

His eyes glittered in the lamplight. "I want to let the storm inside."

Her eyes narrowed, not understanding until he slid from inside her, crawled off the bed and padded to the window. She reached quickly for the lamp and turned it off, just as he whipped back the curtains and flung up the bottom pane. Hot, wet wind blasted inside. Light gleaming from the bathroom wouldn't be enough to let the neighbors see inside.

"The floor will get wet," she muttered.

He glanced over her shoulder. "Do you really care?"

"Guess it depends on whether you're planning to distract me." She laid down the challenge, loved the hard curve of his mouth as he stomped back to the bed.

His hand darted out, grabbing a pillow. She started to roll away, but he stepped onto the bed, bracketing her between his feet.

She stared up, her gaze snagging on his thick, hard cock, bobbing high against his belly. "Come down to me," she whispered, rising to her knees.

He dropped, causing the mattress to bounce. She aimed a glare, tucked her damp hair behind her ears then bent toward his straining sex.

His fingers gripped her skull, guiding her, taking charge, aiming her down, beneath his cock. She stuck out her tongue and flicked it at his balls. He kept them shaved, for her. Something she appreciated as she swiped the velvet sac. His hands forced her closer and she opened her mouth, engulfing his hard stones. Everything about him was hard, so damn masculine. She loved that about him. Reveled in it. All man but still not an asshole. How had she gotten so damn lucky?

Jenna brought her hands into play, gripping his shaft.

His fingers dug into her scalp and forced her mouth upward. She slicked her tongue up his long cock, curled the tip around his corona and then sucked him inside her mouth.

His breath hissed between his teeth, and a smile stretched her mouth. So did his thick cock as she bent over him, taking his length down her throat. Swirling her tongue, she teased him as she fought his grip to rise and fall, sinking deeper and deeper.

Danny gave her hair a stinging pull, tugging her off his cock, then forced her down on all fours in front of him. His fat, blunt head found her entrance, butted against it once, and then his dick sank all the way inside.

She let loose a long, trembling moan and resettled her knees to lift her bottom, inviting him to plunge deeper. A sharp slap landed on one cheek, and she let out a surprised laugh. Another landed and her pleasure gushed to coat the thickness ramming up inside her.

When his calloused thumb pressed against her anus, she let loose a groan. "Oh, please, Danny."

"Want me to stop?"

"Fuck no. Jesus, that feels so good."

His thumb pushed inside, a burning stretch that had her pussy and asshole clenching. His hips renewed their hard, sharp movements, slamming his lower belly and groin against her, slapping sweat and leaking pleasure, echoing the pulsing, wet wind that washed over them.

The moment felt elemental, destined. A silly sentiment if she'd thought about it any other time, but the man straining behind her, pounding into her, was a hard, buffeting force, his breaths coming in ragged gasps and chopped groans to match her own shuddering sighs.

When her orgasm consumed her, she almost cried out a complaint because she was nearing the end. But the strength of it stunned her, curling tightly inside her core, pulsating outward toward her limbs until she collapsed against the bed.

They lay in a tangle, his body blanketing hers. A kiss landed on her shoulder. "I don't want to leave."

"Then don't. Ever."

"Could get complicated," he murmured.

"When is it anything else?" She reached back a hand and caressed his cheek. "Lie with me."

"I should close the window."

Jenna shook her head against him, her lips curving. "I like storms."

Danny smiled, pulled free and spooned his body around hers. They both faced the window with its billowing curtain. Everything precious lay inside his grasp. A feeling of homecoming, of hope for a happy future, eased away the last of the fear and anger that had ridden his body throughout the night.

He slid his hand between her legs, cupping her sex, feeling possessive and pleased.

Jenna let out a deep sigh, and her breaths evened out in sleep.

Outside, the wind died down, and the last jagged white forks descended from a pitch-black sky.

ABOUT THE AUTHORS

MICHAEL BRACKEN, an award-winning writer of fiction, nonfiction and advertising copy, is the author of almost nine hundred short stories, several of which have appeared in Cleis Press anthologies.

SIDNEY BRISTOL is a recovering roller derby queen, former missionary, and tattoo addict. She grew up traveling the rodeo circuit with her parents. Sidney has lived abroad in Russia and Thailand, working with children. She now lives in Texas where she splits her time between a job she loves, writing, and reading.

BRINDLE CHASE, an award-winning and best-selling author, brings us worlds of rapid action and smoldering love from a unique perspective as a male author. His sexy stories of contemporary and paranormal erotic romance and erotica will melt your E-reader.

CHRISTINE D'ABO loves exploring the human condition through a romantic lens. She takes her characters on fantastical journeys that change their hearts and expand their minds. When she's not writing, she can be found chasing after her children, dogs or husband.

ADELE DUBOIS is a multipublished author of erotic romance. Before turning to fiction, Adele wrote for newspapers and magazines in the United States, Caribbean and United Kingdom. Adele and her real-life Navy hero husband enjoy their eastern Pennsylvania home where she is working on her next novel.

TAMSIN FLOWERS, a naughty girl on a journey of self-discovery as an erotic writer, is as keen to entertain her readers as she is to explore every aspect of female erotica. Hoping to touch you on your most erotic zones, she writes lighthearted stories that are sexy and fun.

SHARON HAMILTON loves all things paranormal: angels, dark angels, watchers, guardians, upogenie and vampires. She also has developed a series of hot romantic suspense Navy SEAL stories. Her characters follow a spicy road to redemption through passion and true love—not exactly what they taught you in Sunday School!

TAHIRA IQBAL took a very early retirement from the film and TV industry to follow her passion and true calling for writing.

ELLE JAMES spent twenty years livin' and lovin' in South Texas, ranching horses, cattle, goats, ostriches and emus. A former IT professional, Elle happily writes full-time, penning adventures that keep her readers begging for more. When she's not writing, she's traveling, snow-skiing, boating or riding her ATV while concocting new stories.

ALICE JANELL is a romance author who enjoys hoarding more yarn than she can knit with. Alice is currently living in Okinawa, Japan with her daughter and real-life romance hero husband: a bagpipe-playing, kilt-wearing marine. She promises she's not making him up.

JENNY LYN is a writer of naughty stories and a lover of all things Southern. She's a published author and contributor to the anthologies, *Best Women's Erotica 2013* and *Felt Tips*.

MACY MAN was a true Southern belle, until she discovered the delicious world of erotic romance. Now she pens racy romances to please a reader's heart, mind and body.

LEAH RIDGEWOOD became a storyteller in bed while she lay awake imagining how her most improbable fantasies could come true. She lives with her husband in San Francisco, where her kinky and quirky *Sex in San Francisco* series is set.

SABRINA YORK, Her Royal Hotness, writes naked erotic fiction for fans who like it hot, hard and balls-to-the-wall, and erotic romance and fantasy for readers who prefer a slow burn to passion. Publishing in multiple genres, Sabrina loves writing all kinds of hot, humorous stories.

ABOUT
THE EDITOR

DELILAH DEVLIN is a prolific and award-winning author
of erotica and erotic romance with a rapidly expanding reputation for writing deliciously edgy stories with complex characters. Whether creating dark, erotically charged paranormal
worlds or richly descriptive historical and contemporary stories
that ring with authenticity, Delilah Devlin "pens in uncharted
territory that will leave the readers breathless and hungering for
more..." *(Paranormal Reviews)*.

Ms. Devlin has published over a hundred and twenty erotic
stories in multiple genres and lengths. She is published by Atria/
Strebor, Avon, Berkley, Black Lace, Cleis Press, Ellora's Cave,
Harlequin Spice, HarperCollins: Mischief, Kensington, Running
Press and Samhain Publishing. Her published print titles include
*Into the Darkness, Seduced by Darkness, Darkness Burning,
Darkness Captured, Down in Texas, Texas Men, Ravished by
a Viking* and *Enslaved by a Viking.* She has appeared in Cleis
Press's *Lesbian Cowboys, Girl Crush, Fairy Tale Lust, Lesbian*

Lust, Passion, Lesbian Cops, Dream Lover, Carnal Machines, Best Erotic Romance (2012), Suite Encounters, Girl Fever and *Girls Who Score.* For Cleis Press, she edited 2011's *Girls Who Bite*, and 2012's *She Shifters* and *Cowboy Lust.* In 2013, she'll be adding full-length titles published by Montlake Romance.

More from Delilah Devlin

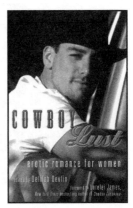

Cowboy Lust
Erotic Romance for Women
Edited by Delilah Devlin

There's a reason Western romance never goes out of
fashion—cowboys are undeniably sexy. "*Cowboy
Lust* is a bevy of hot, hard cowboys ready to give you
more than an eight-second ride. Believe me, you
don't want to miss this collection."
—Beth Williamson, author of *Hell for Leather*
ISBN 978-1-57344-814-7 $15.95

Smokin' Hot Firemen
Erotic Romance Stories for Women
Edited by Delilah Devlin

"Firefighters are damned sexy. Live
vicariously and read all about their brave,
gorgeous selves in Delilah Devlin's
rapturous romance collection. Get your
fire hose ready in case these guys get just
a little too hot to handle."
—Jo Davis, bestselling author of the
Firefighters of Station Five series
ISBN 978-1-57344-934-2 $15.95

She Shifters
Lesbian Paranormal Erotica
Edited by Delilah Devlin

"The always exhilarating author Delilah
Devlin knows exactly what her readers
want—daring, erotic, and wickedly
delightful stories filled with amazing
characters, exciting story lines, passion,
and an abundance of emotions that will
keep them riveted to the pages."
—The Romance Studio
ISBN 978-1-57344-796-6 $15.95

Many More Than Fifty Shades of Erotica

Please, Sir
Erotic Stories of Female Submission
Edited by Rachel Kramer Bussel

If you liked *Fifty Shades of Grey*, you'll love the explosive stories of *Yes, Sir*. These damsels delight in the pleasures of taking risks to be rewarded by the men who know their deepest desires. Find out why nothing is as hot as the power of the words "Please, Sir."
ISBN 978-1-57344-389-0 $14.95

Yes, Sir
Erotic Stories of Female Submission
Edited by Rachel Kramer Bussel

Bound, gagged or spanked—or controlled with just a glance—these lucky women experience the breathtaking thrills of sexual submission. *Yes, Sir* shows that pleasure is best when dispensed by a firm hand.
ISBN 978-1-57344-310-4 $15.95

He's on Top
*Erotic Stories of Male Dominance
and Female Submission*
Edited by Rachel Kramer Bussel

As true tops, the bossy hunks in these stories understand that BDSM is about exulting in power that is freely yielded. These kinky stories celebrate women who know exactly what they want.
ISBN 978-1-57344-270-1 $14.95

Best Bondage Erotica 2012
Edited by Rachel Kramer Bussel

How do you want to be teased, tied and tantalized? Whether you prefer a tough top with shiny handcuffs, the tug of rope on your skin or the sound of your lover's command, Rachel Kramer Bussel serves your needs.
ISBN 978-1-57344-754-6 $15.95

Luscious
Stories of Anal Eroticism
Edited by Alison Tyler

Discover all the erotic possibilities that exist between the sheets and between the cheeks in this daring collection. "Alison Tyler is an author to rely on for steamy, sexy page turners! Try her!"—Powell's Books
ISBN 978-1-57344-760-7 $15.95

Red Hot Erotic Romance

Obsessed
Erotic Romance for Women
Edited by Rachel Kramer Bussel

These stories sizzle with the kind of obsession that is fueled
by our deepest desires, the ones that hold couples together, the ones that haunt us and don't let go. Whether just-
blooming passions, rekindled sparks or reinvented relationships, these lovers put the object of their obsession first.
ISBN 978-1-57344-718-8 $14.95

Passion
Erotic Romance for Women
Edited by Rachel Kramer Bussel

Love and sex have always been intimately
intertwined—and *Passion* shows just how
delicious the possibilities are when they
mingle in this sensual collection edited
by award-winning author Rachel Kramer
Bussel.
ISBN 978-1-57344-415-6 $14.95

Girls Who Bite
Lesbian Vampire Erotica
Edited by Delilah Devlin

Bestselling romance writer Delilah Devlin
and her contributors add fresh girl-on-girl
blood to the pantheon of the paranormal.
The stories in *Girls Who Bite* are varied, unexpected, and soul-scorching.
ISBN 978-1-57344-715-7 $14.95

Irresistible
Erotic Romance for Couples
Edited by Rachel Kramer Bussel

This prolific editor has gathered the most
popular fantasies and created a sizzling, no-
holds-barred collection of explicit encounters in which couples turn their deepest
desires into reality.
978-1-57344-762-1 $14.95

Heat Wave
Hot, Hot, Hot Erotica
Edited by Alison Tyler

What could be sexier or more seductive
than bare, sun-warmed skin? Bestselling
erotica author Alison Tyler gathers explicit
stories of summer sex bursting with the
sweet eroticism of swimsuits, sprinklers, and
ripe strawberries.
ISBN 978-1-57344-710-2 $15.95

Unleash Your Favorite Fantasies

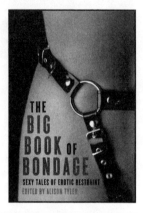

Fuel Your Fantasies

Carnal Machines
Steampunk Erotica
Edited by D. L. King

In this decadent fusing of technology and romance, outstanding contemporary erotica writers use the enthralling possibilities of the 19th-century steam age to tease and titillate.
ISBN 978-1-57344-654-9 $14.95

The Sweetest Kiss
Ravishing Vampire Erotica
Edited by D. L. King

These sanguine tales give new meaning to the term "dead sexy" and feature beautiful bloodsuckers whose desires go far beyond blood.
ISBN 978-1-57344-371-5 $15.95

The Handsome Prince
Gay Erotic Romance
Edited by Neil Plakcy

A bawdy collection of bedtime stories brimming with classic fairy tale characters, reimagined and recast for any man who has dreamt of the day his prince will come. These sexy stories fuel fantasies and remind us all of the power of true romance.
ISBN 978-1-57344-659-4 $14.95

Daughters of Darkness
Lesbian Vampire Tales
Edited by Pam Keesey

"A tribute to the sexually aggressive woman and her archetypal roles, from nurturing goddess to dangerous predator."—*The Advocate*
ISBN 978-1-57344-233-6 $14.95

Dark Angels
Lesbian Vampire Erotica
Edited by Pam Keesey

Dark Angels collects tales of lesbian vampires, the quintessential bad girls, archetypes of passion and terror. These tales of desire are so sharply erotic you'll swear you've been bitten!
ISBN 978-1-57344-252-7 $13.95

Best Erotica Series

"Gets racier every year."—*San Francisco Bay Guardian*

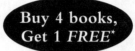

Best Women's Erotica 2012
Edited by Violet Blue
ISBN 978-1-57344-755-3 $15.95

Best Women's Erotica 2011
Edited by Violet Blue
ISBN 978-1-57344-423-1 $15.95

Best Women's Erotica 2010
Edited by Violet Blue
ISBN 978-1-57344-373-9 $15.95

Best Bondage Erotica 2012
Edited by Rachel Kramer Bussel
ISBN 978-1-57344-754-6 $15.95

Best Bondage Erotica 2011
Edited by Rachel Kramer Bussel
ISBN 978-1-57344-426-2 $15.95

Best Fetish Erotica
Edited by Cara Bruce
ISBN 978-1-57344-355-5 $15.95

Best Lesbian Erotica 2012
Edited by Kathleen Warnock. Selected and
introduced by Sinclair Sexsmith.
ISBN 978-1-57344-752-2 $15.95

Best Lesbian Erotica 2011
Edited by Kathleen Warnock.
Selected and introduced by Lea DeLaria.
ISBN 978-1-57344-425-5 $15.95

Best Lesbian Erotica 2010
Edited by Kathleen Warnock.
Selected and introduced by BETTY.
ISBN 978-1-57344-375-3 $15.95

Best Gay Erotica 2012
Edited by Richard Labonté. Selected and
introduced by Larry Duplechan.
ISBN 978-1-57344-753-9, $15.95

Best Gay Erotica 2011
Edited by Richard Labonté.
Selected and introduced by Kevin Killian.
ISBN 978-1-57344-424-8 $15.95

Best Gay Erotica 2010
Edited by Richard Labonté. Selected and
introduced by Blair Mastbaum.
ISBN 978-1-57344-374-6 $15.95

In Sleeping Beauty's Bed
Erotic Fairy Tales
By Mitzi Szereto
ISBN 978-1-57344-367-8 $16.95

Can't Help the Way That I Feel
Sultry Stories of African American Love
Edited by Lori Bryant-Woolridge
ISBN 978-1-57344-386-9 $14.95

Making the Hook-Up
Edgy Sex with Soul
Edited by Cole Riley
ISBN 978-1-57344-3838 $14.95

★ **Free book of equal or lesser value. Shipping and applicable sales tax extra.**
Cleis Press • (800) 780-2279 • orders@cleispress.com
www.cleispress.com

Ordering is easy! Call us toll free or fax us to place your MC/VISA order.
You can also mail the order form below with payment to:
Cleis Press, 2246 Sixth St., Berkeley, CA 94710.

ORDER FORM

QTY	TITLE	PRICE

SUBTOTAL	
SHIPPING	
SALES TAX	
TOTAL	

Add $3.95 postage/handling for the first book ordered and $1.00 for each additional book. Outside North America, please contact us for shipping rates. California residents add 9% sales tax. Payment in U.S. dollars only.

★ **Free book of equal or lesser value. Shipping and applicable sales tax extra.**

Cleis Press • Phone: (800) 780–2279 • Fax: (510) 845–8001
orders@cleispress.com • www.cleispress.com
You'll find more great books on our website

Follow us on Twitter @cleispress • Friend/fan us on Facebook